IN ELEVEN STORIES, *The World With Its Mouth Open* follows the inner lives of people in Kashmir as they navigate the uncertain terrain of their days, fractured from years of war. From a shopkeeper's encounter with a mannequin, to an expectant mother walking on a precarious road, to a young boy wavering between dreams and reality, to two dogs wandering the city, these stories weave in larger, devastating themes of loss, grief, violence, longing, and injustice with the threads of smaller, ordinary realities that confront the characters' lives in profound ways. The stories, even as they circle the darker aspects of everyday living, are—at the same time—an attempt to run into life, into humor, into beauty, into another person who can offer refuge, if momentarily.

Zahid Rafiq's *The World With Its Mouth Open* is an original and powerful debut collection announcing the arrival of an important voice that bears witness to the human condition with nuance, heart, and incredible insight.

the world with its mouth open

the world with its mouth open

stories

zahid rafiq

TIN HOUSE
PORTLAND, OREGON

This is a work of fiction. All of the characters, organizations, and events portrayed in this novel are either products of the author's imagination or are used fictitiously.

First US Edition 2024
Printed in the United States of America

Manufacturing by Sheridan
Interior design by Beth Steidle

Library of Congress Cataloging-in-Publication Data

Names: Rafiq, Zahid, 1986– author.
Title: The world with its mouth open : stories / Zahid Rafiq.
Description: First US edition. | Portland, Oregon : Tin House, 2024.
Identifiers: LCCN 2024025340 | ISBN 9781959030850 (paperback) |
ISBN 9781959030928 (ebook)
Subjects: LCGFT: Short stories.
Classification: LCC PR9499.4.R337 W67 2024 | DDC 823.92--dc23/eng/20240724
LC record available at https://lccn.loc.gov/2024025340

Tin House
2617 NW Thurman Street, Portland, OR 97210
www.tinhouse.com

DISTRIBUTED BY W. W. NORTON & COMPANY

1 2 3 4 5 6 7 8 9 0

for

How about if I sleep a little bit longer
and forget all this nonsense.

—FRANZ KAFKA,
The Metamorphosis

Contents

THE BRIDGE • 1

CROWS • 21

IN SMALL BOXES • 37

BARE FEET • 53

BEAUTY • 66

FLOWERS FROM A DOG • 81

THE HOUSE • 89

DOGS • 109

THE MAN WITH THE SUITCASE • 126

THE MANNEQUIN • 148

FROG IN THE MOUTH • 167

Acknowledgments • 176

the world with its mouth open

The Bridge

FROM THE SECOND-FLOOR WINDOW OF THE CREAKY WOODEN building, Nusrat could see the man's back, his hair, and a shade of his face. She couldn't see the dogs, though, even as they kept on barking. Waiting for the receptionist to call her name, she went on looking out, at the man on the bridge, at the cramped alleyways, at the corrugated roofs of the old houses, at the dark smoke rising from the baker's shop. This was her first time here. A distant cousin had mentioned this clinic a few days ago at a gathering mourning a relative. "I was going mad," the cousin had whispered. She had a two-year-old daughter now.

From the cousin's sketchy directions, Nusrat had found her way up here early in the morning, by guesswork and doggedness, and by asking an old man in a tracksuit for the school the cousin had mentioned as the landmark. She could see the school now, across the street, the red brick building silent and forlorn, its small rectangular courtyard empty.

The man was still standing against the banister, his back to her. He wore a faded blue shirt. She watched him. Was he catching fish? Wasn't it too early in the day to fish? Or maybe this was when people did it. She would need to eat more fish now, that was what the hakeem had just told her, as he had checked beneath her eyelids and her tongue and felt carefully with his cold, unhurried fingers below her navel, around the little belly. He had mentioned other things, black carrots, spinach, nuts, almonds, milk, but on fish he insisted. "Eat well," he had said, "and do not worry too much, and do not skip on the medicine." Now, waiting for her medicine outside the hakeem's small room, she wondered again if she had enough money, for the medicine, for the fish, for the ride back home. She counted in her head and, to make sure, looked into her bag. Everything put together, she had enough, unless the medicine cost too much. She knew where she could buy fish. It wasn't far, she could walk there. And after that she could take an auto-rickshaw home. Or maybe she should take the bus. Auto would be easier, but how it would jerk and rattle. The bus was better that way, and cheap, and there might even be a vacant seat at this morning hour. But what if it got crowded later? Heads, arms, legs, bodies against bodies, no place to take a breath, and again she remembered the vomit and the cramped seat of the bus, the pale dirty pool between her feet, the putrid smell, even though it had been three weeks now. "It is okay, okay," her husband had said, holding her forehead as she wiped her mouth with the corner of her dupatta. How she had wanted to vanish from that seat. How embarrassed her husband's face had looked. She remembered the other faces in the bus, and her mouth soured, a faint nausea swamped her senses.

Leaning her head out of the window, she breathed in a long breath. It felt good to breathe. She breathed again. She could see the man's hands now. He wasn't catching fish. Both hands gripping the railing, he was just looking at the water. Nusrat heard her name called, finally, and she walked toward the counter.

Two small pouches of fine powder, one white and another gray, a pinch from each to be mixed every evening in warm mustard oil and applied around the region of the navel. "Slowly," the man said, moving his hand over the light sweater that stretched against his belly. The hakeem had already explained this to her, but she didn't mind the tired-looking receptionist repeating it. His hand traveling in small circles, she wondered how long it would take her to grow to his size. He opened another pouch, showing a dark green herb, like tea, a half spoon to be dropped every morning in lukewarm water. Not stirred, just dropped in and allowed to sit for five minutes. "Drink only as much as you can in three gulps," the man said. "Three?" she asked, awakened. "Three," the man answered.

The stairs were still dim, and she held on tightly to the railing, as she had on her way up. One plank at a time. It was the right thing to do. The first time, she hadn't been so careful. Not that she had been careless; she had just been a healthy twenty-eight-year-old woman pregnant three months after marriage, just as it was supposed to be. The first time had come as a shock. She returned from the hospital with her hand on her belly for the whole of the ride. The doctors said she was young, and everyone cheered her up, blaming a barren aunt's evil eye, a sister-in-law's envy, a beggar who had one day left cursing, and amid the care and attention and the hope of her own youth she got over the loss. The second time, though, for weeks afterward she still felt the baby inside her. She knew it wasn't there, and yet something in her kept count of the days and weeks. She couldn't bear people the second time, she wanted to go away, walk deep into corners and disappear. How cautious she had been the second time, done everything right, and yet it had lasted fewer weeks than the first. The doctors again spoke hopefully, and the family blamed others, her husband was kinder to her, at times like a stranger. Endless days spent at clinics and afternoons cried away at shrines, asking beggars to pray for her. Pills in the morning, pills in the day, pills at night, pills that swelled her face, thinned her hair, parched her lips. Smiling anxiously at children, asking them to come to her, she discovered around her, in shrines, in clinics, in the neighborhood, in her own family, a breed of childless women who, it seemed, had not existed before. Two years and eight months after the second miscarriage she was finally carrying again, and this was the farthest she had yet come.

IT WAS BRIGHT OUTSIDE. The air felt warmer against her face. She sat on the landing, her legs somewhat parted, her back resting against the wall. She brought out a banana from the bag. The medicine was cheaper than she had thought, unlike at the doctor's, where they took all her money at every visit, this test and that test and bags full of medicine. More people were walking on the street now: two men, a woman in heels, a teenage girl, a young boy. Had she seen someone a few years ago sit as she sat now, eat a banana like that, she might have looked away in embarrassment. Now she didn't even care. The boy was looking at her. She smiled at him. "Where to, little one?" Nusrat asked. The boy smiled shyly, looked away. His backpack slung across his back, she watched him walk away, toward the bridge. The man was still there, and from the landing he suddenly looked like Rajaji, her friend Saira's brother. But Rajaji had been thin, and this man wasn't, and yet somehow he resembled him. She watched him carefully. He was Rajaji, the same height, the same hair parted on the side, but what would Rajaji be doing here in the morning, standing on the bridge? It was not him.

She could have gone left, the way she had come, but she made her way toward the bridge, even crossing over to the same side. She would quietly pass him by, whether or not he was Rajaji, or maybe she could say salaam and ask him how Saira was. What was wrong in that? She had known him well, after all, Saira's elder brother; how he used to make them laugh. As she walked closer, she hoped it was him and became afraid it wasn't. He did not notice her even from three steps away. Her voice startled him. "Rajaji," she said, a smile on her face. It was him. Something strange lay in his eyes, something distant and cold. His face frightened her. "I am Nusrat," she said, "Saira's friend." Uncertain, she smiled wider. "Don't you recognize me?" For a moment she thought he had lost his mind, but he didn't look mad. Or maybe he was not Rajaji.

"Baybi," he said. "You have grown."

Now she smiled at the name Baybi, which was what she had been called at home till she got married. "You have also grown," she answered.

"I have grown old," he said.

No, you look the same, she wanted to say, but she couldn't. So she asked about Saira. How was she?

"Fine," he said. "She is fine."

"That is good," Nusrat said. "Thank God."

He was still far away, but not like at first when he had turned to her. Then, he hadn't even been there.

"Where were you?" he asked. "Is your in-laws' home around here?"

"No," she said. "I had some work, nearby." She wanted to leave, go her way. "Is everything fine?" she asked. "Everyone fine at home?"

"Yes, thank God. Everything fine. Everyone fine."

"How is Saira's daughter? Did God send her anything more?"

"Yes." He nodded. "A son. Eleven months old now. The girl is growing up. You girls grow up so quickly."

His lips trying to pull into a smile, she could see him now.

"Did God send you anything?" he asked.

"Not yet," she replied.

Rajaji did not answer. He looked toward the water, one hand still wrapped around the railing that came to his waist.

She, too, looked at the river. Dirty water ran in quick currents, cutting into one another, the reflection of the bridge broken in the currents.

"Are you waiting for someone?" she asked, turning to him.

He looked about vacantly for a moment and then took his hand off the railing. "Yes," he said. "I had to meet someone, a person . . . for some work."

The face she remembered was somewhere in his face but another face, looser and saggier, had taken its place. Small pouches hung under the eyes; the eyes themselves seemed to have receded.

"Are you going home?" he asked.

"Yes," she said. "But I need to buy fish first." She didn't need to say it, she didn't know why she did.

"Fish?" he asked.

"Yes."

"You should get them in the market near the culvert."

"Yeah, that's where I am going."

"Yeah." He nodded. He looked at her, smiled briefly, then looked down again.

"Say my salaam to Saira," she said. "Will you?"

"I will."

"Don't forget."

"I won't."

She walked away. Questions rose in her head. Had he gotten married; did he have children? What about that old aunt of theirs who couldn't walk, was she alive? She wanted to turn back, to see if he was still there, but she was afraid he might be watching her walk away. Was he still working at the glass shop, hadn't he often spoken about starting his own business? What business was it? She couldn't remember.

She turned immediately when she heard her name called—"Baybi, Baybi"—and was surprised to see him walking toward her with long strides. He must have forgotten to say something, she thought.

"I will also come with you," he said. "I, too, have to go that way."

They walked in silence, took the right toward the main road. What about your meeting, she wanted to ask, but she did not. Shopkeepers rolled open shutters around them; some swept patches outside their stores. She wanted to say something, but she was not sure what. Two soldiers in motorcycle helmets stood with their guns pointing at the street, a half-empty bus trudged past, the young conductor beckoning them in.

"Come this way," Rajaji said. "It is quicker, and less traffic."

They turned into a narrow lane paved with stones. On both sides were old houses, their small windows opening right on the alley, carrying out voices from inside and the smell of bread. When the alley narrowed even more, Nusrat fell a step behind, walking watchfully on the slippery stones that had been smoothed over the years. She looked at Rajaji's shoes, old and misshapen but still sturdy, the soles thick. She would like shoes like that. Her own paper boats were no good for walking, making her back ache in ten minutes.

"What were you doing there, Rajaji?" she asked. "On the bridge?"

"Nothing," he said. "Just standing, waiting for someone, but then I thought he wouldn't come. If he was to come, he would have already."

She wanted to ask more, but she couldn't. He was, after all, Saira's brother, and she hadn't seen Saira in years. Now she felt strange even walking with him. What would someone think if they saw them together? What would her husband think? She watched him walk ahead of her; he had put on weight, he had aged. When was the last time she had seen him, spoken to him? She couldn't remember.

"Rajaji," she said. "Do you remember the day you fell from the pear tree?"

He half turned toward her, nodded a little. "'Up, up,' you both kept saying, and I too a fool."

"We thought you were going to die." She smiled.

"God saved me that day," he said. "Those were different days, Baybi."

She hadn't thought about those days in a long time, they had remained too far behind, and it seemed as if they hadn't actually existed, as if they had been part of someone else's life, someone she had once closely known and then forgotten. But now, she started remembering more things, their home, their conversations, the afternoons she had spent there with Saira.

"Those eggs you used to make," he said. "Green with chilies. The tongue would burn."

She had forgotten she had ever cooked at their home. But she had, and it was strange that he remembered those wretched eggs with five or sometimes even six green chilies. It was things like that which had ruined her stomach. Now chilies were forbidden to her, she couldn't touch pickle, even her salt had been cut down; now food tasted like water.

They turned right into another lane, wider than the last one, where a few small shops were beginning their day. He walked slower, till they were next to each other. A copper seller arranged pots on top of one another, a jeweler looked at them passing by as he wiped his window glass, and just ahead a woman said "Hosshhhhh" and threw a pail of water on the path in a great swish. Nusrat rose on her toes and tiptoed over the rushing film of water, and yet her feet got wet, a feeling that was surprisingly pleasant.

"Did you get married, Rajaji?" she asked as they turned into another narrow lane.

"No," he said. "Not yet."

"Why not?"

He lifted his right hand, palm up, and she watched it linger in the air between them, and then the hand sank back, a gesture she did not understand.

"Why not?" she asked again.

He turned to her, smiling. "There should be some unmarried people too."

Why? she wanted to ask. And why you? But she did not. Instead, she thought about his age. He had been six or seven years older than them, so he must be, what? She counted in her head: forty-one, forty-two. It wasn't old for a man, he could still find a wife.

The smell of fish hit her all at once, a smell of forgotten damp rags. They walked through the busy street toward the culvert, and as they got close, a fisherwoman called to her, while another stood up to motion them over with an extended arm. "Absolutely fresh," the first one shouted, "by God and his prophet. Fished out just this morning." "Come come," the other said, "come and see. I won't, God forbid, force you into buying."

That was the problem with buying fish, the talking, the haggling, the feeling afterward that you had somehow been cheated. It wasn't like buying chicken or meat; fish were different. "Buying fish is a skill," her mother used to say, "and only women can do it, men can't tell between a fish and a snake." But unlike her mother, she was no good at it. She wasn't good even at touching it, at looking behind the fish's ear for the pink, a mark of freshness according to her mother. Fish were too strange, too slippery.

"How much for a kilo?" she asked the fisherwoman.

"First you see," she replied, holding up a fish twice the size of her hand. "Seeing is for free. Then we can talk money. I won't, God forbid, steal from you."

Nusrat tried to see behind the fish's ear, and the fisherwoman, noticing the tentativeness of her touch, flipped it herself.

"See. If this is what you are checking for. But it is not behind the ear that you find anything. Let me show you."

The woman brought out another fish, dark and shiny, and turned its mouth toward Nusrat. Between the fisherwoman's small fingers, a round mouth opened, with lips thin like old people's lips. "See," the fisherwoman said. The fish was alive. Nusrat looked at the tub where she now saw fishes wriggling, slipping, turning against one another in the water. A little fish tossed up from the tub and fell right back in, its body jerking sharply between the others, lapping up water with its tail.

Amid the smell and the sight and noise of the market Nusrat sensed the nausea returning. She moved aside and asked Rajaji, who was standing beside her, to get it for her. The fisherwoman looked at her, a sharp knowing glance, and then turned to Rajaji. "The way I treat you, may God treat me the same. If you don't thank me at home when you eat it, come and spit at my face tomorrow and say, 'Aunt, this is what you deserve.' I will be right here."

Nusrat watched Rajaji looking at the fish the woman weighed on the scale and she knew that her mother had been right. If her mother were alive, she would have bought this fish. How different would things have been? She could have gone to her mother's home and lain down and behaved even more tired than she was and slept for a long time, and when she got up, the food would have been ready.

"See. Lest you say I gave you less!" The fisherwoman held the scales toward Nusrat. "At least one hundred grams more."

"I wouldn't say that." Nusrat smiled.

"Do you want them cleaned? I won't charge. Only for you."

"Yes, please," Nusrat said. "Thank you."

The woman cleaned the fish with a small dark knife. Nusrat watched her fingers run back and forth on the fish so quickly, one moment at its tail and the next at its head, turning it to one side and another, and then suddenly the tip of the knife entered near the throat, the blade twisting up briefly. Something snapped inside. The woman picked another fish, and the dark blade and her thin fingers covered in shining scales kept going up and down, cleaning away the little green fragments of glass.

"Most people don't know about fish," the woman said, without looking up. "The ones I dislike are those who pretend, poking here and there, and in the end they only fleece themselves. I watch and say: 'Good for you.'"

Nusrat tried to smile, but what she wanted was to leave. She took the money out from her bag, but Rajaji said he would pay. Nusrat said no. Rajaji insisted, the fingers of his right hand going in his pocket. Without looking at him, Nusrat handed the woman money. Rajaji looked down, the fingers remaining in his pocket.

Rajaji offered to carry the fish, but Nusrat said they weren't heavy. She walked quicker than before, trying to get away from the smell tugging at her insides. She should slow down, not go so fast. "Let me carry them," he said. She thought about it, and she would have liked not to carry the bag with the fish, but she did not feel right in giving it to him.

"You are all grown up now," he said. "When you guys used to ask for all those Pepsis, then you were not embarrassed."

"It was different then," Nusrat said, remembering the Pepsi and the chips they would sometimes ask him to buy, knowing that he had very little money. She slowed her step. Even though the smell wasn't there anymore, it lingered within her.

"I see you the same as you were," Rajaji said. "Talking, talking, Saira and you, endlessly, phis, phis, phis, phis . . ."

She felt removed, she wanted to be alone, she wasn't sure it had been a good idea to buy fish. She should have asked someone else to get it. She breathed a deep breath, then another, to displace the nausea, but she felt sick, her mouth tasted sour, her legs were tired. Rajaji, too, fell quiet. Now that she had the fish, it wasn't clear where they were walking. The traffic was getting dense and loud. She felt this urge to be back in her room, to lie down and rest for a bit, and then she could have thought about what to do next. Rajaji walked, looking near his own feet, the stubble around his jaw full of grays and whites. Now when she saw him from so close and knew that he was Rajaji, she did not recognize him at all. For one moment she was convinced he was not Rajaji. How had she even recognized him earlier?

"Baybi. Are you okay?"

"Yes," she said, looking away, suddenly aware of her own face, the dark spots, the thinning hair. "I am just thirsty."

"I will get a bottle of water," he replied. "Or would you like to have yogurt laess instead?" He pointed to somewhere ahead on the street and said there was a good milk seller in there.

She was unsure about drinking on the road, but she was sure that it would help her more than the water. "Yes," she said.

THE MILK SELLER filled the tall copper glasses to the brim, so full that it was inevitable some would spill as she picked it up. He sprinkled a pinch of crushed mint on the top and gave the first to her.

The glass was ice-cold, and when she raised it very to her lips, the liquid, too, was cold, but fresh, with the whiff of mint and a hint of salt. She needed it.

"Do you have something to eat, tchot, chochwor, anything?" Rajaji asked.

"I used to," the milkman answered, pointing to the empty wicker basket in the corner. "But with age I can't do it all by myself."

"Is the baker nearby?" Rajaji asked.

"Yes, in that lane behind you."

Rajaji put down his glass and said he would be back in two minutes. Nusrat said she was fine without a bread, but if he wanted to eat he should get it, not for her, though. The truth was she hadn't eaten anything this morning except the banana, and she was hungry. She watched him walk away and turn left. By the time he returns, she thought, the laess won't be so cold either.

She leaned against the wooden electric pole, taking some weight off her feet, which were sore near the heels. Her lower back, too, had a tinge of soreness, something that she knew would grow into an ache if she did not rest in time.

"Here, daughter, sit on this." The milkman passed her an old wooden stool from inside. She thanked him and sat. Her feet and back were relieved. She held her back straight and gently stretched it. What would someone think if they saw her sitting on the stool, drinking outside the milkman's shop? One of her brothers, maybe, or her husband, or maybe one of her mother's brothers? Would they be surprised to see her there? She could say that she was thirsty. It wasn't like she was committing theft. One gets thirsty, especially in this condition. But what if Rajaji came at that moment with the bread? What would they think? No one would think anything. She wasn't an eighteen-year-old girl anymore. But she should go home after this, she needed to be careful, needed to rest, and then she could iron the clothes and, later in the afternoon, cook the fish. With collard greens and radish, yes. But without chili they would come out so bland. Better just fry them. At least they would be crisp.

She took a little sip from the drink, her fingers getting wet from the water that had formed on the glass. She brought out a handkerchief from her bag and dried her fingers.

"How far is the baker?" she asked the man.

"Just here, in the lane," he said. "But one has to wait for one's turn. But it shouldn't take him much time," he added. "He just needs two."

She watched the lane that Rajaji had walked into. Someone walked in or out every now and then. At some point, for no reason, she told herself that he was going to come at the count of ten, something she had not done in a long time, counting time like that. Under her breath she began. "One. Two. Three. Four. Five. Six . . ." At six she closed her eyes, leaving only an opening for a quivering of light. "Seven, eight, nine, and ten." She kept her eyes closed for a moment, and when she opened them, the lane was empty, he wasn't there. She smiled at the silliness.

Drops of water slipped down the tall glass, just as they had on those Pepsi bottles that she saw clearly now. She had never understood where the water came from, believing for a long time that it oozed from the inside, but then she knew better, and yet she had never found out where it really came from.

"It shouldn't take so long for two breads," the milk seller said quietly.

"Maybe there are a lot of people," she said.

"Yeah, but still! He just needs two."

"Should I take a look?" She set her glass next to Rajaji's on the marble sill. Just as she took the first step she turned back and asked the milk seller if she should pay him first, and seeing that he was unsure even though he said that money wasn't going anywhere, she insisted with a smile and placed the money beside the glasses. "I will be back," she said, and walked away, her bag slung on her shoulder and in the other hand the polyethylene bag with the fish.

Two men and a woman stood outside the baker's shop, their backs toward her. One of them, she thought, was Rajaji. But then he turned, a stack of lavaas in his hand and a cigarette stub in the corner of his lips. It wasn't him. She walked closer, peered into the baker's shop. Except for the baker and two apprentices, no one was inside. She looked around, not really knowing what to say, and when one of the apprentices asked her what she wanted, she mentioned Rajaji. Had he been here? A man, wanting two breads? Fifteen minutes ago?

"People come for two breads all the time," he said, a smile glinting in his eye.

An arm stretched above Nusrat's head, extending a cloth bag. "Ten," the man said, "six crisp and four soft, and don't be a miser with the poppy seed."

"He was wearing a faded blue shirt," Nusrat said to the apprentice. She wanted to say, too, that he had a few days of stubble on his face and that his hair was parted on the side, but she didn't.

The apprentice did not know, but there was another baker in the lane ahead to the left, he said; he might be there.

Walking there, she wondered if Rajaji might be back at the milk seller's by now. He could have passed by while she was at the baker's, her back to the street. But it made more sense to check at the other baker's now and then return to the milk seller. He would wait there if he was back, she thought. She hoped he had better sense than to set out looking for her.

A group of people stood outside the other baker. The sight of so many people gave her hope. He was there, she said to herself, annoyed that he had not got the bread from the first baker where fewer people were waiting. From one stranger's face she looked at another's. Her heart began to sink. He must be inside. Why would he be inside for two breads, though? She asked a teenage boy for space so that she could look inside. She wasn't buying anything, she told him, only looking for someone. His eyes on her face, he moved aside.

Inside, people sat in a haze of smoke and only after focusing her eyes for a moment could she see them. One by one she scanned the faces. The bitter smoke stung her eyes. Rajaji wasn't there. She looked again. Where could he have gone? She wanted to ask about him, but there was a conversation going on, and she could not bring herself to it, and so very feebly she whispered to the man pulling bread out from the mouth of the furnace if someone had come asking for two breads. He turned to her for an instant, his face glowing in the light of the fire, drops of sweat on his forehead, and then he turned back. He didn't know, he said, and in the curved hook of the slim dark iron rod he brought out another bread, and then another, and another, laying them beside him in a heap.

The boy who had made space for her asked if she had found him. No, she said. There was another baker ahead, he said. Maybe he was there. Not the one in this lane—he pointed to where she had come from—but that way.

She looked where his finger pointed. "How far is it?" she asked.

"Not far. Five minutes, walking. On cycle it takes only two."

His directions were precise, involving a left and a right and then another right, and crossing in the process into another neighborhood, past a small mosque, an army bunker, a walnut tree.

She thanked him but said she would first check at the other baker's again. Maybe he was there. She started walking, knowing the boy was looking at her and feeling as if she was doing something wrong.

"These elders," the boy said after her, "they have no shame, they fleece children of their turn. Children shouldn't be sent to the baker."

At first she thought he meant it about himself, but then she understood that he might have thought that she was looking for a child who had gone to buy bread but had not yet returned. There was no one outside the first baker, and Nusrat did not look inside. She hoped that Rajaji would be back at the milk seller's by now. In her mind she saw him sitting on the wooden stool she had been sitting on, waiting for her to return, the two breads in his hand. She was hungry, and she was annoyed, and if she didn't check herself she could see herself scolding him. When she turned right to the milk seller's she almost saw him, but instead there was a woman talking to the milk seller. The stool was not even there.

"Did you find him?" the milkman asked.

"No," she answered. "Did he not come back here?"

"No," the milkman said.

Noticing that she was looking for the stool, he handed it to her again. Nusrat sat down. This time she needed to sit.

"Did you look at the other baker?"

"Yes," she said.

"Was everything fine around there?" he asked. "Something hadn't happened, God forbid?"

Nusrat said no with a nod of her head.

The glasses stood on the sill as she had left them, except for a page that covered them both.

"For flies," the milk seller said. "This one is yours."

She took a sip, but it no longer tasted good. Like water and yogurt and salt. She was hungry. She could have at least bought herself a bread, how foolish, how foolish the whole thing. More than hungry, though, she was tired. For the first time it occurred to her that Rajaji might not return. She knew she could take an auto and go home. That would be the best thing to do. But where could he have gone? Did she miss him at the baker's amid the smoke? She had looked at each face there. Should she have gone and looked at the other place the boy had mentioned? But why would he go so far? He had been strange when she had met him, but then he had been fine. What if he had an accident? I hope the soldiers did not take him. But then someone would have seen something, they would have said something at the baker's.

"Why don't you call him?" the milk seller asked. "Don't you have a phone?"

"I don't have his number," she answered.

"Oh," the man said. "Can't you call someone at home and get his number?"

"Yes."

"Is everything fine?" the older woman standing there paying for cheese and yogurt said.

"Yes," Nusrat said.

"The man with her, he went to the baker," the milk seller said. "Left his glass here, barely touched it, and it is almost half an hour, he's not back."

The woman looked at Nusrat with sympathy, and suspicion. "Did you have a fight?"

"No," Nusrat said.

"Don't worry. He will be back," the woman said. "If my husband or sons are ten minutes late, my heart is lost. You hear stories, your heart is lost. Did you look properly at the baker's?"

Nusrat wanted to leave, but she felt embarrassed leaving behind the drinks and walking away when the milk seller and the woman were so concerned. If he came back, she thought, she would not speak to him. She would just leave. She wouldn't even touch his bread.

"Times are bad," the milk seller said. "One hand doesn't know about the other."

"Call someone, get his number," the woman said.

"Do you want to use my phone?" The milk seller held out a small black phone, a thin streak of yogurt along its side.

"I have a phone," Nusrat said and brought out her phone from the bag. Without really seeing she scrolled through the contacts and, hovered her finger over the green button. She put the phone to her ear.

"Hello," she said softly. "Asalamalaikum. Yes, I am fine. Yes, yes. I will be back soon." She rose, quietly, trying not to look at them and at the two glasses. She could sense their eyes on her. "I met Rajaji on the way," she said. "Yeah, he is well, yeah, but he went to buy bread. Yeah. To the baker." She moved the phone from her left ear to her right and shifted the fish that seemed to have grown heavier in her left hand. She began to walk away. "Do you have his number? Yes. I did. Okay," she said. "Please. I did. Yes." She turned out of the narrow lane, no longer in sight of the milk seller and the woman, and for several steps she kept the phone against her ear. A man sold ice cream on a cart, a fruit seller stood to her right, oranges and apples and pomegranates sitting in little heaps of their own. She thought about asking for his number from Saira, but what would she say she needed it for, and how would she even get Saira's number? People and names ran through her mind, Tanzeela, Yusra, Afroza, they might have Saira's number, but who would give her their numbers?

She stopped in front of the busy square. Looking at the faces around, she wondered if Rajaji could be somewhere on that very street. She was tired and hungry, and her feet and back ached, and under the bright sun she felt as if she had left home a long, long time ago. The boy's directions rang through her head, and she wondered if she should have gone to look for him at the other baker's. Again, for no reason, she felt that he would come right there, to the road where she was. But how would he even know she was there? At the milk seller's it made some sense, but here? And yet, this time she was surer when she closed her eyes.

"One, two, three, four, five, six, seven, eight, nine . . . nine . . . nine . . . nine . . . ten."

In dizzying brightness people walked in all directions, a scooter came toward her, a car went the other way, and buses passed huge on the road, the sun glinting off their bodies and their mirrors and glinting off the windows of the shops on all sides and the strange noise of so many voices and vehicles rising together as if everything were fused, everything together, going somewhere, going everywhere, going nowhere, at the same time. Someone touched her shoulder, tugged at her, and, her hand reaching for her belly, she turned. A man was standing behind her, pointing with his hand toward a car with a man leaning his head out of its window, honking the horn, terribly, and shouting, "Do you want to die?"

Crows

EIGHT MINUTES HAD PASSED, ANOTHER SEVEN REMAINED. IT was only a matter of time. And yet the boy went on running his pen just above the paper, to keep the calamity from striking before its hour.

The three other pupils sat in the other corners: legs crossed, heads bowed, writing. Or were they pretending as well? May that be the truth, the boy wished, casting a quick glance at the teacher, who sat behind the low wooden desk, looking into a thick book.

Last evening the boy had been so close to learning the functions of the liver. He had sat down in a corner of his parents' room with the book in his lap when a faint voice murmured in his heart: *Let's do it in ten minutes.* That page with the diagram of the liver remained open all evening while he wrestled with his cousin, who called himself the Rock and could lift his eyebrow just like the wrestler. In their thick woolens they grappled and struggled, each trying to pin down the other, letting out battle cries, till they fell exhausted on the floor. On his back, looking at the flaky green ceiling, the boy tried raising his eyebrow like his cousin, like the Rock, but both his brows kept going up, which was strange, because it was his cousin's brows that were knit together while his own were far apart. He tried till his eyebrows hurt. Then they were called for dinner.

It was the first question: "Explain the functions of the liver along with a diagram."

If only he had looked at it and then gone to wrestle, he could have written something on the blank page. How long would it have taken? Five minutes? Ten? Now he tried hard to remember what a liver looked like, but all he could see were the kidneys, facing each other like beans, thin tubes coming out of them. Should he just draw the kidneys? Better kidneys than nothing. But what if that made the teacher angrier?

The teacher sat motionless, still staring into the book on the desk. He taught math and science to the higher classes at the boys' school, and in mornings and evenings gave private lessons at home. He was known for his teaching and his beatings, and together they had grown a legend around him. The boys in the tenth grade said he could solve every math problem in a second, the ninth-grade ones said he knew everything in science, and together they agreed that his hands were made of steel and his laser gaze could see through your head. And what added to the legend, too, were the stories of kindness and rare forgiveness, of slapping a boy only to find his face burning with fever and giving him the day off, of charging only half the fees from orphans. The boy stole a glance at him now, trying to gauge his mood, but with his lips pulled tight under the dark mustache, his cheeks clean-shaven, his eyes looking down, the teacher was inscrutable.

Sami, the boy's friend, sat in the corner to the right. The boy watched him blow a mist of white breath at his hands, and then, as if trying hard to remember something, he scratched at his neck. He too seemed stuck. The boy wanted Sami to look toward him, but Sami suddenly bent over the page and began writing. He tried to see if Sami's pen touched the paper. It didn't; or did it? It was too far to tell.

"Are you done?" The teacher's voice echoed in the silence of the room.

The boy turned to him in surprise and quickly looked down.

"Where are you lost?" the teacher asked.

"I was just thinking," the boy answered.

"What is there to think?"

The boy started writing.

"If you have memorized the answers of these questions at home, you will print them on these pages here," the teacher said. "You cannot think their answers now, or can you? Then you would be a genius. Are you a genius?"

The boy slowly drew a vertical line, dividing the blank page into narrow halves.

"Five minutes left," the teacher announced. "I don't feel like beating anyone today. It is too cold, I feel I have a fever. So if you write only two good answers, you should be fine."

"Fission," the boy wrote on one side of the line, and "Fusion" on the other. They had to list four points differentiating the two, and he knew that in fission one broke into two while in fusion the two came together. But that was all he knew. He remembered the teacher talking about the sun, about hydrogen, helium, about the atomic bomb. He remembered the name of the city too, Hiroshima, a name he had immediately liked on his tongue, *Hero-shima*; the name brought along the image of the dark cloud that had stood on the page like a giant tree. He could not, however, remember if the bomb had been the fission or the fusion, and that was all that seemed to matter.

Mildly interested in the teacher's words when they were reading the lesson, the boy had been distracted by the sounds that came from the nearby field. "Pass, pass," someone had been shouting the entire time, and the boy couldn't help but wonder who it could be, playing on such a cold afternoon. Musa must be there, he had thought, and the Rock too; he was sure he had heard Pinku's voice. How lucky they were, he had thought, to be out there, playing! But how did they get to be lucky? How did it work, being lucky? As he thought of that afternoon now while the others went on writing, voices swam into the silence of the room, quietly at first, and then they rose in his ears, Musa's voice, Pinku's voice, the Rock's voice, and slowly he again drifted out of the grim cemented room and onto the vast bright field between the two faraway goal posts. Musa, Pinku, Sami, and the Rock were chasing after the ball. The boy waved his arms at them. They gestured for him to join. And through the vast field he ran, his feet leaping off the hard earth, cold fresh air filling his chest, every stride bringing him closer.

Sami passed him the ball and the boy took off immediately, pushing it with his right foot and chasing after it, picking up speed. He dribbled past the Rock, and as he ran on, the pen stopped moving in his hand, a tingling ache crept through his folded limbs. Left foot right foot left foot again he pushed the ball through Pinku's legs. As he ran closer to the goalpost, Sami came in from the left, yelling, "Pass, pass." And just when he made it into the penalty area, "Three minutes," the teacher announced.

Thinking about playing even now, the boy wondered. What a bastard you are! He will skin you in a few minutes and you are scoring goals.

The third question was from algebra, and he couldn't understand what it asked of him. Even if last night he had learnt the functions of the liver and the differences between fission and fusion, he would never have opened the math book. Math was beyond him, digits and alphabets that meant nothing, *x*, *y*, *x* + *y*, *x*/*y*, and he could not just keep the math book in front of him and dream, as he did with the other textbooks; in math meaningless problems had to be solved with pen and paper, problems that kept him from dreaming. Everything else, a sound, a song, a fight at home, the shape of a cloud, cows grazing in the field, the rain sliding down the glass pane, carried him elsewhere.

He returned with quiet determination to the liver, this time trying to imagine it with his eyes closed. Soft and brown it lay on the round chopping block, with no real shape, and like jelly it shook when the cleaver fell on it. Sometimes his mother sent him to buy the inexpensive meat of the lamb—kidneys, liver, spleen, lungs—and she fried them together for lunch, spicy, with a hint of lemon, and garnished it with chopped coriander. The taste now lingered near his lips as he drew the liver, somewhat triangular, raised in the middle. He shaded it gently with his pen, but stranded in the middle of the ruled white page, it did not look like a liver at all; in fact, it looked like nothing. So he drew under it the round block of wood, and then hanging uncertainly above it, the knife.

One after the other, two boys stood up and handed in their answer sheets. The teacher set aside his book. "For some reason," he said to the two boys, "this hand of mine is itching." He scratched his right palm with the fingers of the left. "Now it could only mean two things."

The boy knew it was about him and so did the two bastards who chuckled away so quietly.

"Either a lot of money is coming my way," the teacher said, "or someone is going to get beaten bad by me. And since money never comes, that leaves only one thing."

Those two must have done well, the boy thought. They always did. Questions with red pen, answers with blue, all written in cursive.

The teacher held up the answer sheet of one of the boys. "Look at this handwriting," he said. "Pearls. Pearls."

It was too far for the boy to glean anything from that page, even the shape of the liver. As always, it took the teacher no time to check their answers.

"One minute!" he said to the two still writing. "It is an easy paper! What is taking all this time?"

Then Sami, his friend, stood up and walked toward the low desk.

"Now remains only one," the teacher said. "I think he is answering all the questions, he doesn't like to leave anything unanswered. Let him. He still has a minute. I will even give him an extra one, special offer only for him."

Sami turned to look at him, asking with his eyes if he was doing okay. The boy could see that Sami had done well. He felt betrayed.

He thought of handing in his paper and submitting to whatever lay ahead. What is the point of this, anyway? Whatever is going to happen is going to happen! Why wait? Better to get it done with. But what if something happened in this minute? What could happen in a minute, though? The teacher's sister could come in with her sick baby and together they could rush to the doctor. Or the soldiers could barge in again in their big boots, turning everything upside down, poking even into their schoolbags with the long guns. But even the bastard soldiers wouldn't come today. Maybe the Rock could come! Riding his bicycle, breathing hard, saying that the boy was needed at home, immediately, that something had happened, that his mother had fallen sick; the boy saw her lying on the narrow bench in the clinic, her big hand fallen senselessly to the side.

The sharp sound of a slap woke the boy. He looked up and found Sami holding his face in his hands.

"Is *this* isotope, and *this* isobar?" the teacher asked Sami. "Where are your brains begging when I am teaching?"

Isotope? Isobar? A sudden panic ran through him. The boy had never heard the words before. It went quiet in the room, and the teacher turned toward him. Without knowing what, he began to write in a flurry.

"Bring it now," the teacher said. "Let it be."

THE TEACHER STARED at the boy's face while he tore his answer sheet to pieces and then he flung those pieces at him. Even before the drifting squares had settled on the low desk between them, he struck him twice across the face. The boy's ear buzzed, his face stung. Sami and the two boys lowered their heads into the books.

"Stand up," the teacher said.

The boy began to rise, his gray tweed pheran coming down to his calves. He mumbled that his mother had fallen sick.

"I know," the teacher said. "Today it is the mother. Yesterday it was the father. Tomorrow it will be the sister. I know you now."

The teacher picked a square of torn paper and spat on it. A frothy little spittle, the same color as the paper. He held it out to the boy and placed it on the dark wooden desk. "This is your clock," he said. "Before this dries, you must be back. Or I will cut out your liver and show you what it looks like."

THE TIP OF his nose numb, the boy walked around the teacher's yard. His breath hanging near his cold face in little white clouds, he looked behind the overgrown hedges, between the sacks of sand stacked against the wall, behind the run-down tin shed. Two sticks, long and thick, lay on the pale dead grass behind the shed. He tried them on his hand, leaning first toward one, then the other. They would break his bones. He hid them inside two tall bushes and scampered toward the pomegranate tree, looking for something smaller. Yellowed dead leaves lay under his feet, as if someone had scattered them quietly. A crow cawed somewhere. He looked up, at the electric wires, at the tin roofs of the houses, at the bare trees. A crow cawing, his grandmother said, meant someone was coming. But no one's feet approached the rusted grille of the gate. The gate stood still. What if he left? The thought occurred suddenly to him. He saw himself slipping out, the gate closing without a sound behind him, and the long road outside. At once it seemed possible, real. He *could* do it, but at once fear filled him. He stood in the yard, looking at the gate, barely seeing it. Where would he go? Home? Wouldn't the teacher be at his home in ten minutes? Wouldn't he be beaten worse, and by everyone? What about his grandmother's? He could go there. He could walk. He pictured a mob entering his grandmother's gate, sticks in hand, shouting for him. Where would he go then?

He had never wanted to come here for lessons. It was his mother who had brought him early one morning, pulling him out of sleep, saying she was unwell and needed him to accompany her to the compounder. Just before they got to the teacher's home, he knew where he was being taken. Sami had told him about the beatings. Even worse than at school, he had said. But he had also said that the teacher did not accept everyone, and that early morning, as the teacher's sister led the boy and his mother into the warm kitchen, his hopes had rested on being refused. The teacher's old mother had poured them tea. "He will come down soon," she had said. "From morning till evening he teaches, and by evening he is exhausted. Falls asleep in that corner, sometimes doesn't even eat." The boy looked at the corner, at the mangled red cushion that lay there, finding it hard to imagine the teacher curled up there, refusing to get up for dinner, just as he did at his own home sometimes. "Missed medical by three marks," the teacher's mother whispered. "And the next year his father died. Would have been a big doctor today. But!" She sighed and ran her fingers across her creased forehead. "Fate."

The teacher had asked him two questions, and even though he knew the answer to one, the boy remained quiet. No one spoke in the kitchen. Only the boy's mother had whispered, "Shame, shame." The teacher refused him. But then his mother begged everyone in the kitchen. She said the boy never studied, that he was lost, interested only in playing and staring at things. He would remain illiterate, she had said, end up a laborer or a salesman, and the world would trample him under its feet.

"The boys who study here are very good," the teacher said. "He will not fit in."

Her hands pressed together, tears streamed down her face. "I have come with hope," she said. The boy had been dreading his mother's tears, how they came every time she needed them.

"Don't cry," the teacher's mother said. "He is a young boy. He will study."

The teacher asked the boy to look up and for a long moment stared into the boy's eyes, and without wanting to, the boy looked back at the master's face, at the little scrap of bloody red paper stuck to his unevenly shaven throat.

"You should know one thing." He turned to the boy's mother. "He might return home weeping tomorrow."

"Beat him, skin him, pull out his nails. But please give him education. We have little money and our home is no good for studies. His cousins go to school when they feel like, but their fathers at least make money. He will be ruined. For the sake of God, save him from ruin. I will pray for you five times a day."

You pray only in the mornings, the boy wanted to say, and that too only when you need something.

"Send him from tomorrow," the teacher said. "With all his textbooks. And remember about the crying. Some boys study happily, some weep through it."

THE STICK BALANCED on his right palm as if his hand were the center of a weighing scale, the teacher smiled at the boy. "What is this?"

The boy remained silent, his head down.

"Sami," the teacher called out. "Is this a stick, or is it a matchstick?"

Sami did not answer.

"I mean, look at this and then look at him. Do you think it is worthy of him?"

Sami looked at the thin pomegranate switch on the teacher's palm but did not turn to look at his friend. He stared back into his book.

"What were you doing outside all this time, rathead? Hiding the real sticks? Ten people must have been killed in the city since you left. And you bring me back this? Even this paper is dry."

The boy had already sneaked a look at the paper, finding a hint of the teacher's spit still on it.

"Go stand against the wall," the teacher said. "And take off these duvets that you have layered yourself with. Keeping yourself warm and cozy."

The boy remained motionless. And then a few moments later he walked over to the wall. Holding the collar of his long pheran, he pulled it over his head. Underneath, he wore a maroon jacket. He prayed for the zipper to get stuck. It came down smooth. Sparks cracking in his hair, he pulled off his sweater. In a checkered shirt and gray trousers he stood against the bare mildewed wall.

"Will we wait for you till evening?" the teacher shouted.

The boy stood motionless, his arms hanging loose at his sides.

The other children buried themselves deeper into their books. Someone turned a page; its crackle cut across the room.

"You are wasting everyone's time," the teacher shouted, and in three mighty strides he was grabbing at the boy's collar. The boy began to beg. "Of all the sticks I have left there, you bring me a limp twig." He started unbuttoning the boy's shirt. "You think me a fool?"

Clutching at the ends of his unbuttoned shirt, the boy was crying. "Please, please." He folded his hands. The teacher undid the buttons at the boy's cuffs and tried to pull at the shirt. "Let it go," he said. "I said let it go." The teacher's hand swung against his face, his brains shook, and the shirt came off.

He ran around the small room, finding himself again and again in corners. He begged as he ran, howled for one last chance. A thousand sticks fell sharp on his thin arms and his bare back, his neck, his head, his cold fingers, his numbed feet. The other boys shrank, their bags pulled tight against them, leaving more space for him to run. And he ran, and he wailed, and the louder he wailed, the harder the stick fell, till exhausted and removed from his own skin the boy no longer felt the blows. He wasn't even running anymore, just huddled in a corner, shielding his head with his arms. The teacher kicked him in the shoulder, kicked him in the back, kicked him in the legs, and then flung the stick at him. The beating was over. In the silence of the room the boy whimpered like a little dog.

The teacher walked toward the window and, reaching behind the curtain, returned with a newspaper with tall green grass in it.

"No, no," the boy yelled, his body alive again. "Not the nettle. Please. Not the nettle." He began to sob. "I will bring a bigger stick. I will bring two. I know where they are."

He crouched behind the other boys and, from there, begged for a last chance. The others looked in silence at the teacher, walking toward them holding the nettle in the newspaper like a bouquet.

"Come out from there," he said calmly. "The quicker we do it, the faster it will be done. Don't make me angrier with your sly tricks."

The boy leaped toward the door and in one desperate lunge pulled it wide open, but then he stopped. Better to be beaten here than in the kitchen. The teacher grabbed him by the hair and slashed at his back with the nettle and rubbed it against his shoulders and his arms and his throat.

"You come here to ruin my class!" he shouted. "You pimp! And you think I will let you?"

The boy went on yelling, drowning the teacher's words in his cries. The teacher held the boy by his thin sideburns and jerked him to attention, his face inches from the boy's. "Do you know what is waiting out there?" he said. "Do you?" The skin on the boy's face felt on the verge of tearing as he looked at the master's distorted face.

"The world," the teacher yelled. "With its mouth open. You hear me? With its mouth open."

THE BOY SAT by the door where the beating had ended. A thousand little ants dug their burning teeth into him. He pressed against the freezing wall and it cooled the embers on his back for a few moments.

The teacher was behind the desk again, drinking water from a plastic bottle in which big bubbles rose. "Nothing happens to him," he said to the other boys. "Only I get tired." He blew air at his hands that stung from the nettle. "A dog's tail put a hundred years in a rod came out crooked still."

Someone pushed at the door. The boy moved. The teacher's sister peered in.

"You woke her again," she said to her brother, pointing at the baby whimpering in her arms. "Now I have to walk her around with my broken back."

She craned her neck in and looked behind the door. "I knew it was you," she said to the boy. "Your wails come in my nightmares now."

"But nothing happens to this dog," the teacher said.

Hiding himself with thin naked arms, the boy did not look up. The baby cried louder. The boy resisted the urge to scratch at his burning skin. The sister entered the room.

"Forgive him now," she said to her brother. "Let him wear clothes. He will fall sick."

"To hell with him. It is all useless," he said. "He will be happy to fall sick and sit home. He will not study. No point wasting time and money on him. He will be better off working at a mechanic's place. Will learn some skill early on."

She gathered the boy's clothes strewn across the room. Sami passed her the checkered shirt that had fallen near his knee.

The teacher threw the bottle of warm water at the boy. "Drink," he said. "You are a waste of time. A rock. On which nothing will ever grow. Bring your mother with you tomorrow, and your father too. I will speak with them."

The boy drank while the teacher went on speaking. "Of all people I have met in my life," he said, "this guy can become a cold-blooded killer. Don't go by his innocent face. He is a criminal inside." Bubbles gurgled away in the bottle in the boy's hand. "If you run an X-ray on his chest, you will find a rock in there. A black rock."

THEY WALKED ALONG the uneven dirt road fenced by willow trees and tall thickets and barbed wire. Neither Sami nor the boy spoke. Behind the trees and the tangles were patches of empty vegetable gardens, and in the distance occasional sad-looking houses, their tin roofs drawn low over their faces.

Rising on his toes, Sami reached for a berry, pinching a tremble through the clump; down below, hanging from the barbed wire, someone's faded black shoe twirled slowly.

"Are you in pain?" Sami asked as he pressed the red berry between his thumb and forefinger.

"Not much," the boy whispered.

"But how could you not learn even today?" Sami asked. "He had said he would kill you if you failed this time. Hadn't he?"

They neared the small plum orchard that they sometimes sneaked into when the trees were full with fruit, returning with their pockets filled with plums so red that they looked black. Not a leaf on them today, the trees stood still, their bare arms raised silently toward the sky.

"Why didn't you learn?" Sami asked again.

Though they walked beside each other, the boy seemed far away.

"Tell."

"I tried," the boy said. "Yesterday evening, and then this morning, too, but I couldn't do it. I just didn't feel like doing it, reading, learning."

"Who feels like it?" Sami said. "Nobody feels like doing math and learning science, except those two testicles, maybe. I do it only to avoid the beating. Everyone does it because of the beating."

Without a muffler, the cold air cut into the boy's nose. He cupped his palms around his mouth and exhaled long warm breaths.

"What will you tell at home?" Sami asked. "He said he would beat you on the street if you didn't bring your father and mother. I think he will."

If he told at home, the boy knew he would be beaten again. And he couldn't go back tomorrow without his father and mother. His hands still around his mouth, he turned to the sky where countless birds flew across the vast dim grayness.

"I think you should tell at home," Sami said. "Maybe this is the end of it. Or maybe tell them tomorrow. That way you won't be beaten again tonight."

Beating their wings and gliding, the birds descended, then rose high, cawing together a great noise that filled everything.

"Where do these crows go every evening?" the boy asked.

Sami looked up at the sky, then looked at him. "Wherever," he said. "What does it matter where they go? What matters is what you tell at home tonight, and whether you are going to be beaten again."

He knew Sami was upset with him. He felt the agitation in Sami's voice, but there was no agitation within himself. His body was still stinging, but his mind was calm, as if it had been emptied of everything.

"Where do you think they are going?" he asked again.

"To their nests," Sami replied. "Where else?"

"But why return every evening when they could just go on flying?"

Sami looked into the sky. "Where would they spend the night if they don't return to the nests?"

"They could stay in the nests of those ahead of them," the boy said, "and the ones behind could stay in their nests. And they could keep going."

Sami looked on at the sky. "But where would they be going?"

The boy thought about it for a moment. "I don't know," he said.

An old man emerged from behind a tin gate. He walked ahead of them, bent over a tall stick, a creature with three legs.

"He went mad today," Sami said. "I thought he would spare you when you hid behind us. The bastard had brought nettle."

The boy did not answer. He turned back to the birds, no longer a vast dark river but a smattering across the gray sky.

“What will you do now?” Sami asked.

Far away a loudspeaker crackled to life, and a broken old voice called for the dusk prayer. A frail orange glow started to waver in the windows of the houses. Another loudspeaker went off somewhere. Then another. They no longer heard the birds. Darkness thickened around them; with uncertain steps they walked slowly. The crows became sparse, flying now in ones and twos, the empty sky growing between. The boy looked on into the fading light.

In Small Boxes

ONE OF MY GREAT DESIRES DURING THAT TIME WAS TO PURchase something from Mr. Hussain's store. I was a young city reporter, traveling in overcrowded public buses, smoking cheap cigarettes, frequenting little tea shops, and occasionally buying a book. At the beginning of each month I tried to save some money, only to find myself borrowing modest sums back at the end. Far from being able to buy Mr. Hussain's papier-mâché artifacts, I could only look around his shop, and for not closing his doors on my empty-pocketed desire I greatly respected Mr. Hussain.

Mr. Hussain's store occupied an old colonial building, its faded white walls framed with exquisite shawls and antique rugs. Day after day I found myself climbing up its discolored wooden stairs, holding on to the sleek dark handrail; for hours I ambled through the aisles and the gallery, staring at the boxes, the lampshades, the mirror frames, and the numerous other objects of sheer beauty lining the long wooden shelves. I knew where everything was, the letter openers, the coaster sets, the antiques locked up behind glass displays. From the gallery I wandered into the softly lit hall neatly arranged with dark walnut furniture: writing desks and low armchairs, dining tables and daybeds. I touched everything, felt the carvings with my fingers, felt the smooth surfaces of the wood, and sometimes when Ramzan, the old man who worked at the store, was not there, I furtively sat on the rocking chairs and the sofas.

During these visits I often ran into Mr. Hussain. He stood mostly at the tall window in the gallery upstairs, smoking and looking out at the river. Sometimes he was outside the store, sunning himself on the Bund or walking along that quiet embankment that curled beside the water. Every time I greeted him, Mr. Hussain nodded at me, but we rarely spoke. I had in fact never seen him speak much, except, at times, to the white customers at his store. With them he spoke in impeccable English, about the patterns on the rugs, the grain on the furniture, the colors of the papier-mâché, and why he couldn't lower the prices. Mr. Hussain had spent a few years in England, and it showed in the way he spoke and the way he wore his clothes—light wool jackets in spring and long warm coats in winter, and scarves soft as cotton. No one I knew dressed like him, and even though I imagined him to be in his sixties I thought him the most elegant man in all of Srinagar. It was not just the clothes but a deeper elegance that reflected in everything he did, from the way he held the cigarette between his fingers to the way, lost in some far-off thought, he watched the river, and most of all in the way he let me wander through his store, knowing from the beginning that I was not going to buy anything.

One afternoon, walking beside the shelves in the warm, carpeted gallery, I came across a box the size of my hand. A single red flower was painted on it, and against a pale background the flower appeared on the verge of flaring up. I had never seen the flower before, neither in the store nor in the city's gardens. I looked around for Ramzan to ask about the flower, but he was busy on the other side, cleaning a tray of papier-mâché eggs that he had once told me were Easter eggs, neither of us really knowing what Easter eggs were, except that they had something to do with the Christians.

"The man who painted it is dead now," Mr. Hussain said from the window at the far end.

I wasn't sure he had spoken to me, but after a brief silence he said that there would never be poppies like that again. I tried to show grief at the news, but he went on gazing out of the window and I returned to the newfound poppies with great interest. Touching the lacquered surface of the box, I turned it over. Scribbled on a tiny sticker was a price equal to almost two months of my salary.

"Sometimes," Mr. Hussain said, "one wants to hide oneself in these boxes. Never to be found again."

It was a strange image, Mr. Hussain lying stretched in the small box in my hand. Had I heard him right? I remember looking at him in that moment as he looked out of the open window down at the Bund and across at the river. Clean-shaven, his hands in the pockets of his gray pants, he turned toward me, and I felt that he was going to say something more. He said nothing. And for some reason, it is that afternoon I remember as the beginning of the terrible things that happened afterward.

MY OFFICE WAS not far from Mr. Hussain's store. It lay close to the same Bund that I loved to walk along, passing under an expanse of the branches of chinar trees, and passing the two old magnolias whose hundreds of purple flowers appeared like birds about to take off from the branches. I had, over time, learned not to see the three bunkers between Mr. Hussain's store and my office, and even when I did see the two or sometimes three guns pointing out, I paid little attention. I turned instead to the languid river that, despite being dirty, glinted in the afternoon sun, and at the snow that glimmered on the far mountaintops. I peeked into the courtyards of old restaurants that smelled of appetite and tables laden with rich food and I wondered who these people were, eating all this good food. Lovers sat on benches in the shade of trees, stood by the railings gazing at the water and at each other, in no hurry to get anywhere. I watched them holding hands, humming slight tunes, smiling, complaining, crying, and sometimes suddenly bursting out into explosions of laughter. Even at this drawn-out pace I would be at work in twenty minutes.

I hated entering that concrete building with windows that stared out at the walls of other hideous buildings. Plain plywood desks occupied the damp gray of the newsroom, each desktop cluttered with screens and keyboards and wires. The air, musty from being trapped between the cemented walls, smelled of mold and people's feet. At any pretense I slipped outside, feigning to be on one story or another while I loitered on the streets and met with other young reporters from other newspapers who, like me, sought refuge in conversation. We sat in small tea shops, smoked cheap cigarettes, and discussed politics and literature. I did not know much about either, and neither did most of them, so we said whatever came to us, as long as we agreed that Kashmir must become free. For hours every day we spoke, recounting stories that had not made it into the papers, the stories behind the stories, stories so sad, so funny, so true, that there was no place for them in the papers, stories that in their telling and retelling became myths and belonged to no one and to everyone.

Day after day I wrote about the city's decrepit roads, its clogged drains, and the menace of its stray dogs, and sometimes when the senior reporters had the day off, or if the day was too bloody, I, too, was asked to write about the killings and the gunfights. In all these stories I tried to slip in a beautiful line or two. These lines, however, never made it to the page the next morning, the stories reduced to a skeletal form that robbed them of every trace of me. Eventually I stopped reading my own stories and then the newspaper altogether, but I went on loving the job, for the spontaneous life, for the loitering and the sitting at the tea shops, for the unending discussions amid the smoke from the cigarettes that seemed to be a part of the profession itself, and for the way it kept me away from home late into the night, which to me felt an immense freedom.

The only thing I truly hated about the job was the meeting every morning. It was a farce, and all of us knew. And yet we met six days a week, discussing our ideas for the day, beginning our days with half-truths and lies. To walk out from that meeting and head to the nearest tea shop was a relief. And it was while walking out of the meeting one morning that I saw Mr. Hussain in the front office of our newspaper.

He was shouting at the receptionist, a big man known to have eaten two dozen bananas to win a bet with one of the drivers. In front of him, Mr. Hussain seemed like a small animal barking in desperation. I touched Mr. Hussain on the arm, and when he turned to me, I saw a wild old man. His hair scraggly, stubble on his face, he could have walked out of a hospital ward. "Mr. Hussain," I said. "What's wrong?" Frothing at the corners of his lips, he looked at me for a moment, not able to place me. His eyes without the glasses were drowned in his face. "I come to your store," I said. "Don't you remember me?" I made him sit in a chair and asked the receptionist to bring a glass of water.

The receptionist waved his arm and walked out of the room. "Get it yourself for Lord Curzon."

Water seemed to calm Mr. Hussain down, and I saw that he was clutching in his hand a rolled newspaper that I could tell was ours.

"Do you work here?" Mr. Hussain asked me. Even before I could say yes, he said he wanted to meet the editor. He said he was going to sue the paper, put everybody in prison, and ensure that the newspaper never saw the light of the day. I urged him to remain calm and to tell me what had happened.

The pages rustling in his hands, he opened the newspaper, and while he searched through page after page I wondered if I had gotten myself unnecessarily involved in something beyond my means. I was after all a lowly reporter who wrote about drains and dogs. Mr. Hussain pointed to something on the fourth page. The quality of our inside pages was so bad that it took me time to make out what he was pointing at with his shaking finger, and once I saw it, it made no sense.

Inside a small box was a picture of Mr. Hussain, under which it was written that he had breathed his last early on Tuesday morning. He had passed away in his sleep, peacefully. His death, it said, was a huge loss to his wife and his two daughters, and they prayed for the doors of heaven to be thrown open for him. Then there was his address, his phone number, and the names of his wife and two daughters.

"I want to know who is behind this," Mr. Hussain said. "I am alive. For God's sake, am I not?"

I did not know what to say, so I urged him again to remain calm and said that I would try my best to help. The receptionist returned and, taking no notice of Mr. Hussain, walked straight to his desk. I asked him about the obituary, and he said that someone had given the item for publishing yesterday. "I can't go around asking people for death certificates now, can I?" the receptionist said. "We publish a hundred obituaries a day.

Sometimes from the first page to the last the newspaper is nothing but obituaries. How do I know one of them is not dead?" He stood up and walked toward Mr. Hussain. "I apologized to old papa here the moment I understood a mistake had happened. That is what it is, a mistake. Some bastard has played a sick prank. I even offered him tea and biscuits. Ask him, did I not? I told him that he should forget about it and get on with his day, or we could even put another box in there tomorrow saying old papa is, thankfully, alive and talking."

Mr. Hussain rose from the chair. "First of all," he said, "stop this old papa nonsense. I am no fool. I have seen more of the world than you ever will." He said it was no joke, but a plan, a proper plan. He said he had enemies and the newspaper was in cahoots with his enemies, and as he went on speaking, his voice rose along with the color in his face. His phone had not stopped ringing since early this morning; his wife had to be put to bed with sedatives; people were knocking at his door to offer condolences; it was almost eleven and he had not opened his store. Mr. Hussain was shouting again, and little white droplets gathered again by the corners of his thin lips. He demanded to meet the editor.

"Come in the evening then," the receptionist said. "That is when the editor comes."

"I know the likes of you and your bosses." Mr. Hussain slapped at the reception desk. "I want to know who is behind this."

The receptionist ignored him and looked instead at a thin sheaf of papers.

"I am speaking with you." Mr. Hussain pointed at him.

The receptionist looked toward me and asked me to please take him away.

"You talk to me," Mr. Hussain bellowed. "I will not move from here before I get the truth out of your belly."

"This announcement will come true if you keep shouting," the receptionist yelled back, pointing at the newspaper in Mr. Hussain's hand. "The only mistake then would have been the time."

This set Mr. Hussain on fire. He said whorehouses were better than our newspaper.

"Go to the whorehouse then," the receptionist said.

I held Mr. Hussain by the shoulders and tried to take him away. And I told the receptionist to be respectful to him, but I also did not want to cross the line with the receptionist because he had been there for sixteen years and I hadn't even done six months. Besides, the receptionists, the cab drivers, the printer and his apprentices, the security guards, the office boys—you did not want to antagonize them. It was believed in the treacherous interiors of the office that they, along with some reporters and even some of the editors, were the eyes and ears of the chief editor, who was also the owner of the newspaper.

Once we stepped outside, the fresh air quieted Mr. Hussain. Fumbling through his pockets, he brought out a packet of cigarettes. He pulled one out for himself and offered one to me. We stood at the end of the alley lined with several newspaper offices whose interiors were believed to be as treacherous as ours and the quality of whose pages was as bad. I waited for him to say something, but he drifted farther away with each drag.

"Are you okay?" I asked finally.

He took a long last drag and let the stub fall into the narrow gutter that ran along the wall. The water carried it away, its tip that had been fire just now dark and soggy in an instant.

Appearing older than I had ever seen him, more creased and worn out than he had been in anger moments ago, Mr. Hussain reached into his right pocket for another cigarette. "I am fine," he said.

HE RARELY WENT OUT strolling after that day, nor did he stand much in the sun. Mr. Hussain spent more time now in his small office on the ground floor from where he could see who came in and who walked out. I felt on a couple of occasions that my appearance at his store made him uncomfortable, and I asked him one day if my coming there bothered him. He said it didn't and that I should come as often as I liked. I did not tell him that, as much as I came to the store to see the papier-mâché, the furniture, the carpets, I also came to visit him, that though I had nothing to do with the obituary I felt a vague sense of responsibility, maybe because I had seen him in that disheveled state in our office, and maybe because I was the only connection between this place and that. He had met the editor that first evening, and the editor had apologized to him and explained that it had been a mistake. He had offered him back the little money they had taken to run the obituary but Mr. Hussain had refused, saying it was not his money but rather the money of his enemies. I heard this from the receptionist, whom I tried to avoid but who called to me every time I passed by. He said he had seen Mr. Hussain walk out of the office on fire and with his tail between his legs.

Mr. Hussain still wore his linen suits, but something seemed to have changed about his appearance. He smoked more, walked slower through the store, and looked crumpled. Ramzan told me that he now had to remind Mr. Hussain to eat lunch every day, and even then, he said, he left behind more than he ate. At times, Ramzan said, he saw Mr. Hussain very quietly talking to himself.

One afternoon there was no one in the gallery except the two of us. Mr. Hussain was smoking by the open window. I walked up to him. I told him that I hoped he had forgotten about the obituary and treated it as a stupid joke. He should, in fact, be glad that he was alive. He smoked in silence while I spoke, flicking the ash into an old walnut-and-bronze ashtray that I had not seen before. I had a feeling that I was talking beyond myself, but I was enjoying the moment of intimacy. Speaking like an adult, I went on, suggesting a short trip. "A change of place," I said, "might help put it out of your head." He remained silent even after I finished.

"I am a seventy-one-year-old man," he said. "Too old for someone to play a joke on me. Besides, is this a place for jokes?"

He spoke with a calm I had not seen in him since the obituary. He took time with his words, looking at a couple walking on the other side of the river. Pretending to push each other into the river and laughing, they appeared tiny from this distance, holding on to each other's arms and laughing.

"You are going to be a journalist here," Mr. Hussain said. "It is not a small thing. It is no joke. To tell someone's story. To write the truth."

Mr. Hussain drew words from somewhere far away, and I listened intently to them and to the silences that felt too long, full of unspoken words. Muddied water flowed on in the river, the couple kept disappearing into the distance, and weaving strange shapes, the smoke from Mr. Hussain's cigarette seemed to be making its way into my head.

"Truth is hard," Mr. Hussain said. "Offers no solace. I prefer beauty myself. But you, a journalist, in this war, how long can you hide in beauty?"

Mr. Hussain put out the cigarette in the ashtray and turned to the shelves. "On these boxes, on this paper, on these little pieces of nothing, how many hours of work, how many years, how many lives? And how long to burn it all down, to ash? An hour? Two? Three, at most? Three hours, for all the years?"

Even though I had no idea what it was, I had the feeling that a truth was being revealed to me, and for the whole day afterward snatches of his words echoed within me and I felt the beginning of a new bond with him.

That week, Mr. Hussain seemed to regain his old composure. He walked around the gallery checking on things, in clothes that seemed to have recovered their grace. He even stood outside in the sun. One of those days, just about noon, when I should have been in the municipality office making friends with the new deputy mayor, I saw Mr. Hussain staring for a long time at something; unmoving he stood there with his back to me. I had often wondered what he saw when he looked at these objects for so long, and that day, after he left, I took his place. It was a round brass vase, painted in dark ink, as if by a shivering hand, giving a sense of hurriedly fallen evening. A deer was running through the woods, and behind it was a man on a horse, in the man's hand an arrow about to leave the bow. It was stunning, the animals with their legs in flight, the man, his hands, the bow, and unlike everything else in that store. How had I not seen it before? I held the vase in my hand and turned it to see what was on the other side. A deer, a horse, a hunter, evening. It was worth the four and a half months of my salary.

I was there again the next day, and the day after, and after that too, watching carefully each figure in that scene, and trying also to see it with Mr. Hussain's eyes. At some point I felt I was being watched. Mr. Hussain was standing in the far corner. I walked up to greet him, he nodded at me, and after a brief silence he asked if I could come down to his office. I followed him down the wooden stairs, and he closed the door behind me, drew the curtains. Beautiful green crewel curtains. It was the first time I had stepped into his office, everything in there old and beautiful. The shade of a tall lamp glowed softly in the corner, its pale light falling upon its sleek carved body. What treasures must lie around this room! What beauty everywhere!

With his foot Mr. Hussain moved an old box from the corner, sliding it in front of me. Narrower at the base, it widened as it rose, and thin green painted vines with little red flowers climbed all over it. The box was open, filled with crumpled white and khaki papers nestling a smooth black something that was hard to see in the subdued light of the office.

"What is it?" I asked.

"Look," Mr. Hussain said, looking at me.

I took a step closer, bent down. Cold and soft against my touch, it was a bird. I pulled my hand back like I had touched a naked wire.

"It is a dead sparrow," I said. "Why did you put it here?"

"I didn't," he replied. "Someone did."

"Why would someone put a dead bird here?"

"I don't know," he said. "What do you think?"

Mr. Hussain looked at me as if asking me to solve the puzzle.

"Maybe it came in through one of the windows," I said and checked around for a broken pane. "And died here by itself."

"By itself? I don't think it happened by itself."

"Do you think someone came in and placed it here?" I asked.

He remained quiet for a while. "Did you come yesterday?" he asked.

"Yes," I said. "I asked for you, and Ramzan said you had an appointment with the doctor."

"Did you look for me here?"

In a single moment I understood what he was saying. I turned to him in disbelief. "Are you saying I put it here?"

"I only asked if you came in here searching for me."

I couldn't believe it was happening. I wanted to tell Mr. Hussain that he was making a mistake, a big mistake. I wanted to shake him to his senses, but he seemed to have become some other man, someone I had never seen before, not even the man I had seen at the newspaper office.

"Maybe someone asked you to put it here," he said. "Someone came to your office maybe. Try to remember."

"What are you saying?" I shouted.

Mr. Hussain stepped toward me, and I thought that if he slapped me, I would hit him back.

"Listen, boy," he said. "I have always been nice to you. Haven't I? Here! I have something for you."

He brought out from behind him a box, the pale box with the poppy on it. I looked as he tried to push the box into my hands. I pulled my hands away, hid them behind my back.

"Take it. Please," he said. "I know you don't have a lot of money, and I understand. But you, too, must understand that I have a wife, that I have two children. Please tell me who gave this to you."

Fear and rage surged in me, and at the same time I felt pity for him. The way he looked at me, with his old eyes and white hair, he was almost begging. I wanted to shake him and tell him to wake up. But I felt insulted—more than insulted, betrayed.

"What do you want?" Mr. Hussain asked. "I will give you anything you ask. Please just tell the truth."

I said the truth was that he was a coward and I had made the mistake of coming here too often to see him and his store. "I will never come again," I said, turning toward the door. He grabbed my arm and I pushed his hand away. He shouted after me. He said he would go to the police, he would drag me to the court, he would expose me.

Ramzan was standing outside, listening in on the conversation.

Fuck him as well, I thought, storming out in rage and hurt, promising myself never to return there, even if everything in that store burned to ash.

That scene in his office, the box, the bird, his face, everything kept repeating in my eyes. Sometimes he slapped me, sometimes I slapped him back; sometimes Ramzan also came in and together they tied me with a rope; I saw him faint right beside the wastebasket, and sometimes he died in front of me. Night arrived and everything outside the window became dark, and doubt began to form within me, that I actually was involved in the whole thing, that somehow without my own knowledge I had placed the sparrow in the box. But how was that possible? I slept from one nightmare into another, expecting the police to jump the walls of our house, expecting calls from unknown powerful people, expecting all sorts of terrible things. I thought of speaking to a friend who was now a lawyer, I thought of confiding in another reporter, but I was afraid I would end up spreading rumors about myself. So I kept quiet. But I could not forget about it, and the more I could not forget, the more I hated him.

Two days later, just before noon, I saw Mr. Hussain crossing the busy street. I was waiting outside the police station for an appointment about a story. My first thought was to walk away. But why should I hide? I hadn't done anything; he was the one who ought to be ashamed. I stood there on uncertain legs. Halfway across the road he saw me, and he kept walking, slowly, cautiously, looking right and left, his hand outstretched, as if expecting the cars to hit him. Tired and wasted in the fawn suit, he passed me by, smiling with his thin ugly lips a weak, pitiful smile. A part of me felt like smiling back, but I did not. I was not even sure what his smile meant, its meaning becoming apparent to me only after he walked into the police station.

He was there to complain against me. And convinced that policemen were walking out that very moment to arrest me, I left the appointment and hurried away almost blindly, my legs slipping away beneath me. Suddenly it was clear that the police would believe that I had something to do with it; why else would I visit the store every day when I never bought a thing?

The only person I could think of turning to was the receptionist.

Only he would understand, only he, and I hastened to tell him that he had been right, that the old man had gone mad, that he had now turned against me.

In a sliver of sunlight the receptionist stood in the alleyway outside the newspaper office.

"Have a cigarette?" he asked when I was still a few steps away.

So glad was I when he asked for the cigarette that I could have borrowed money to buy him a whole carton. I brought out the one cigarette I had and gave it to him.

He looked at the cigarette, held it in front of his eyes. "Are you a child?" he said. "Smoking these candy cigarettes." He took little suspicious drags and spoke about the patch of sunlight becoming smaller and smaller in the alley, blaming the buildings rising illegally overnight. He spoke about a dull ache in his right side, near his kidney. He spoke about the dowry for his sister's marriage and about other things that I barely heard. When he noticed that I was distracted, he asked if I had fallen in love.

I told him everything. He heard me out in silence.

"This is what happens," he said, "when you hang out with big people, thinking you will become their friend, taking sides against your own."

I said it wasn't like that. He said he knew what it was like.

He moved a step to the left to remain in the strip of sun. "Didn't he stick it in your ass? Do you enjoy it?"

I said I would need his help if the police called me, and I needed him to come with me to explain to my editor.

"Old asshole," he said. "Remember how he shouted here? I was trying to be nice and he went on and on. Motherfucker."

I agreed. Old motherfucker. I said he deserved it. The receptionist's presence gave me relief. I wanted to stay with him all day in that little piece of sun. I met him several times that day and the next, even when it felt strange and, even cheap, spending more time with him in two days than I had in the six months before.

I waited for the police to call, for a lawyer to call, for someone to call, and every time the receptionist saw me, he asked if the call had come, and then he simply looked at me and raised his eyebrows.

Two days passed, three days passed, a week. Slowly, I returned to the teas and the cigarettes and the conversations amid the hovering smoke. I did not speak about Mr. Hussain. I told other stories, and we laughed, my own laughter fraught with a limp fear as if I were waiting for something ominous that had left from somewhere and was on its way, as if I were living on borrowed time.

THREE WEEKS AFTER I had seen him on the street, Mr. Hussain passed away, on a Sunday. Among a hundred other obituaries, we carried his in a small box on the fourth page. The receptionist showed it to me. He had died in his sleep.

"Old papa, gone," he said, passing me a cigarette. "God works in mysterious ways."

Bare Feet

IT WAS THE STUNTED SHADOW OF THE TALL LAMP UNTIL IT began to quiver, and then slowly it wriggled free. After crawling across the carpet, it climbed up the door, and there it stayed, flickering softly like the dark shadow of a distant flame.

"Brother."

The voice did not come from the door, it came from very near, from behind my ears.

"I have come from far."

I tried to jump off the bed, but my body wouldn't move. This is a dream, I told myself, this is a dream.

"Please listen to me."

I yelled out to Father, loud, for him to hear me in the other room, but I had no voice.

"Please don't be afraid, I bring no harm."

A young man's voice, a boy's really. I had the feeling I had heard it before.

"I have been killed."

Wake up. Wake up.

"You are the only one I could come to. Please help me."

I first saw arms, and then legs, and it became clear that stretched along the door was a man's shadow.

"My mother must be going mad. My father broken. My brother will be searching for me everywhere. My sisters must be weeping. But I could only come to you. Do you see me?"

Above the arms were shoulders, and above them the dark stain of a head. My first night home in three years, and I might not have even come had Father been well, had he not refused to come to America even for a month despite my pleas and our arguments. I had come to make him understand that, without Mother, there was nothing here, except war and desolation.

"Do you see me?"

Yes, I heard myself say.

"Please tell them you saw me. Tell them I came to you. Tell them something. Something that eases their pain."

For three years I had hoped to dream of Mother and not once had she come, and now, back in this room, amid these faint gray walls, these curtains, this memory of a home, I dreamt a stranger.

"It is an old house. Not very big, with ivy on the walls."

Was that how it worked then, the dead, unable to find their own, showing up in the dreams of strangers, in houses where no one knew them?

"A narrow alley runs beside the house. Children play in that alley."

Where? I heard my voice again.

The shadow wavered in silence against the door. "I don't remember."

But what place?

"Please. I could only come to you. Tell them something."

And leaving only the dark of the door, he vanished. I waited for the voice, and when it didn't return I got off the bed and walked up to the door, touched it with my fingers, opened it. Nothing. Just the wooden veins of carved leaves. Across the hall, in the other room, Father lay asleep, softly snoring, his arm across Mother's pillow. I walked into the kitchen, poured a glass of water. Disturbed by the sudden light and my feet, cockroaches scurried about the floor, hiding but not completely. I returned to the room, afraid of finding the shadow again, but there was nothing, just the tall shadow of the lamp by my feet. Lonely, I sank into the bed.

I DID NOT tell Father. He asked if I'd slept well. I did, I said. What could I have said? And even if I had told him, he would have half smiled, half shaken his head, or maybe now, in this new life he seemed to have stepped into, carrying beads on him at all times and a prayer mark on his forehead from the prostrations, he might even have said that of course ghosts lived in every house, just as the living did, and gone on to drink his tea, gulping it down with the handful of pills.

He passed me the paper, saying there was nothing in there. "Trash," he said. Mumbling under his breath, moving his head to the incantations. It seemed to me that he was half there and half elsewhere. A retired bureaucrat, of woolen jackets and aftershaves, disfigured now by the mirror of war, he had grown half a fist of white beard and taken to wearing a white prayer cap. Between the cap and the beard, I found it hard to recognize him.

From the barely working phone I called Hassan. The phone rang for a while. And then buried in the noise of the line his voice came from far. How are you, Hassan? There was a moment's pause. "Fine," he said. "And you?" We agreed to meet in an hour, outside my home.

Damp newspapers stood in tall stacks, and cobwebs hung from the flaking ceiling. Water dripped from taps in the bathroom, leaving circles of rust on the white tiles. Half the bulbs burned out and the windows jammed, I walked room after room through decay, waiting for the hour to pass, but it moved so slowly, time dragging against its will. The cockroaches seemed to have gone elsewhere, but the dishes remained in the sink. How differently I had remembered this house, and now that memory, too, was besieged.

Finally, Hassan arrived on the motorcycle, our old RX 100 that we used to ride aimlessly through the city.

We sat by the river, looking at the water. I told him everything, and, being Hassan, not once did he show a sign of disbelief. In three years he seemed to have aged. He had been there when Mother had died but I couldn't come for his brother, and I was afraid my absence had carved a void between us I might not be able to bridge.

"What should we do now?" Hassan asks.

I don't know. What do you think?

"We must look for the home," he says.

Hassan knows this city, better than me, better than anyone I know, but I am wondering if this is the same Hassan. He seems silenced—by grief, by war, by loss, by something I can sense but cannot see—and in his eyes is this quiet searching gaze, searching for what I don't know, making me feel that he is searching for me as well, that he hasn't yet found me. In his eyes I doubt my own arrival. Funny Hassan, full of jokes and anecdotes, not so funny anymore, carrying his dead brother in him, and carrying maybe the dying country too.

We ride beside the roar of the bike's engine, amplified in the silence of the empty streets grieving a massacre. The crisp spring air cuts against our faces; with watery eyes I watch the city go past. The sky is bright and blue, a single white cloud rowing in its sea. There is the country, bright cloud, shaped like a leaf, drifting slowly on its hazy feet. "Keep an eye out for the ivy," Hassan says. He is watching the houses for the ivy, and so must I.

But I can't look beyond the empty streets, the rusty shop shutters, the cratered walls. I have never seen the streets like this, the city like this. For a moment it occurs to me that it is not my city but some other unfortunate city. Packs of angry dogs in littered corners, birds perched on electric wires, a faint stench of rotting meat. In the windows of houses are silhouettes, brief apparitions peering out at empty roads. Neighborhood after neighborhood, desolation. Nothing but bunkers made of sandbags with loops of barbed wire wound around, and from little holes in the bunkers, dark eyes watch you with pointed barrels. They are everywhere, the bunkers, the blind eyes, the searching muzzles. I had heard all this in my absence but to see it is another thing.

SOLDIERS STOP US halfway across a wooden bridge. "Get down," one of them shouts. Another stands behind him, his gun pointed at us. Hassan negotiates. His grandfather is ill, at the hospital, dying. We have to go; we must go. We show our cards, proving our identities, a businessman and a lecturer at a college in America going to see a dying old man. The soldiers look at our cards and then at our faces and then at the cards again. I look away, only to find guns aimed at us from the corner of the bridge, and I glimpse myself for an instant as they must see me, through the viewfinders of their rifles, a chest, a forehead, a throat. I turn away to the river; it quietly ferries trash. Reluctantly, the soldiers return our cards. We get back on the bike, the howl of the engine setting us free. But even after we leave behind the bridge and turn a street, and then another, I cannot get out of my head the sense that we are riding not through the streets of the city, not through neighborhoods, but through the viewfinder of a gun. I feel so distant already from that shadow and whatever it was that I set out for. It cannot be done. How can anyone find the home of a shadow? What was I even thinking? It must have been a dream. How could it not! I should have stayed home, spent time with Father, tried to convince him to come to America. But why did Hassan not say that it must all have been a dream, that such things happen only in dreams? Why did he come along so willingly? Hassan is no fool; is he indulging me, indulging a friend? Cutting in and out of silent streets he rides on, looking around, searching for the house with ivy. I am not sure I am even looking for anything. I just watch, and feel, sitting so close behind him, a familiar warmth. How did the spring of our conversations run so dry? Why did I stop calling him, from wherever I was, to talk about books, films, women, the small successes and heartbreaks? He, too, had never called, letting instead the falling leaf fall, not throwing his hand in the way. But was it he who had changed, or had I quietly moved away when silence fell over him, filling our phone calls too? He hadn't lowered the memory of his brother into the earth, and I couldn't shoulder his grief. To shoulder his grief was beyond me, and he didn't seem to need another shoulder. Or maybe he did. Hassan suddenly brakes, the tires screech. It is dizzying to come to a halt. Beside us is a narrow lane paved with stones. I don't want us to stop.

Far ahead at the bend, children play. They halt as we climb down from the motorcycle, look at us. An old man's mistrust in a child's eyes. I smile at them as we walk close. They turn back to their play. A girl tosses ahead a stone and jumps after it, landing on her right foot in a small box drawn with charcoal. With her bare foot she kicks at the stone gently, it slides into another box.

The children cheer. Each time she jumps, her two thin braids tied with yellow ribbons jump and dance behind her; it needs to be seen, witnessed, recorded, this moment, this girl. I want to stay here and watch them play, and in the little flights of her bare feet forget about the world. She jumps, jumps again, rising with the flight of her feet. Fly, fly, little girl, far from every hand, except that of love, and if that reaches for your ankles, fly out of that too. Hassan greets the children, and they greet back like children. He asks about a house green with ivy. They seem not to understand. He asks if someone has died in the neighborhood or gone missing, a young man. They raise their arms and point at different houses. They speak together of young men, dead from the houses, including the girl's house. Her uncle, she says, the youngest one, who worked at the medical shop. "Does your house have ivy?" She doesn't know. They lead us to a low wooden gate and the girl runs inside.

In the courtyard a woman washes clothes at a tap near the wall. Another hangs them on the clothesline. A child sits in a red plastic tub, turning in his hands an imaginary wheel. The women look at us, we greet them, they mumble back a greeting. They go on looking as if they have been waiting for someone and are unsure if we are the ones they have been waiting for. I am not prepared for this.

Hassan walks around the house, an old mud and brick house with latticed windows, and I would have spoken of its beauty if only that didn't feel so vulgar. He looks at houses around, and I know he is still looking for the ivy. He has more belief in the shadow than I do.

An old man walks out of the door; we walk toward the old man. He shakes our hands. I should have told the shadow that I can't do it, that it can't be done, and maybe he would have understood and both of us could have gone our ways. The old man is looking at me and so are the two women, the girl, the child in the tub, Hassan, a middle-aged man, and the children, who seem to have multiplied behind us. They are waiting for me to say what I have come to say, and again I can't find my voice.

I am a writer, I say. I am sorry.

The old man looks into my eyes and I have a hard time meeting his gaze.

"What do you write?" he asks.

Poems.

The word feels weak in my mouth. The old man smiles, a smile not mocking me but telling me that I am useless to him and useless to the important things in life, to what has become of life. His eyes are ripe with age, his beard white like the beards of those oracles from the fairy tales, and I want to run into his arms, I want to ask him to save me, to save us. A child, nothing but a child, Father would say if he saw me at this moment. A weak man hiding behind words. I feel like a child now as they lead us into the house and guide us through the corridor. The room is packed with people by the time we sit down. They bring his wife, the wife of the youngest uncle. She remains with her head low, cradling a baby.

No one says anything, they just look at me, not even at Hassan but at me, and I want to run away from these faces and these eyes and this burdened silence, and suddenly it occurs to me that the shadow lied to me. I was not the only one it could visit, it had visited others before me, but no one was as naive. They must have told him that they could not find a house without a name, without an address. How did it not occur to me earlier? Hassan touches my arm. They have brought us tea.

The old man offers me a coconut cookie. I politely refuse. He politely insists. The young wife looks up occasionally but says nothing. The baby babbles in her arms. I can see they are disappointed in me. I bring no news, no prophecy, no hope. Even my silence is hollow, an empty bubble floating on the surface of dates and numbers and lists. I want to be out of here, and I am relieved when we get up. They walk us out, and I tell Hassan that we won't go to another home. We have nothing to say. Hassan does not reply. The children follow us to the mouth of the lane where it meets the wider road, and just as we get on the bike, the girl slides her small hand into mine. I feel the pull of her hand and her eyes and I let myself be pulled. We are walking again, a procession of children behind me, behind them Hassan. We walk past the girl's house and go deeper into the lane that narrows with every step, the houses leaning on one another, as if holding one another from falling, from crumbling into heaps of rubble. The girl pushes open a narrow gate on the left and in we walk, one after the other, cramping the small courtyard of the house. It is a tiny run-down house from another age, and the girl has disappeared inside. Hassan looks around with his quieted eyes, in no hurry to be elsewhere. The girl returns and beckons us in. We walk in through the corridor, whose floor beneath worn-out mats is broken.

A woman lies flat on the bed. Her eyes are open, but she does not look at us. I have no idea what I am doing here, in someone's home, someone's bedroom, so far from my life in our home in the affluent part of the city and immeasurably far from the life I am trying to make for myself. The woman stares at the open window behind us, from which the noon sun falls on her pale face. Another girl stands beside her. Her face lit up against the light green wall, she looks at me with her big bright eyes. The girl who brought us here is beside her, they seem close even though they don't speak a word. She must be the daughter. Hassan speaks in whispers with a man sitting in the corner. I do not want to sit. I say hello to the friend and smile at her, but she does not smile back. She goes on looking at me with her big eyes. Hassan comes up beside me and holds up an X-ray film. It is the image of a spine. He points at a small dot next to the fourth vertebra. "Too close," he says. "Can't remove it." Smaller than a dime, barely discernible amid the smoke of the spine and the ribs, is the bullet. I might never have found it on my own even if I knew it was in there somewhere. The woman lets out a muffled groan. She bites on her lower lip, attempting, I think, to move her body. Her eyes open wide, the teeth sink in deeper. The daughter braces the woman's shoulder and her head. The woman's face tightens, her jaws clench. Exhausted, she sinks back on the pillow, closes her eyes. She has hardly moved. We shouldn't be here. We have no business to be here. I nod at Hassan, suggesting that we leave. He does not move. I make a move to leave, and just then she opens her eyes, and from a great distance she looks at me. I look back at her and find my gaze drowning in her eyes, and I realize that all I have been doing since morning is looking at people's faces and into their eyes. Tears fall down the corner of her eye. We go on looking at each other and I can't understand what she asks of me, but I swear on my mother's grave that she does ask something. They are all asking something and I can't understand what, but I know that it can't be asked in words, the loose change of words that seems no longer of any value in this country.

I think of pressing some money into her listless hand or tucking it under her pillow before we leave, she must need it for medicine, for her daughter, for this life, but I am afraid money is too easy, it will ruin everything.

While I put on my shoes, Hassan quickly walks back in. He has forgotten the keys, he says. The girl who led us here is holding hands with the woman's daughter. No one speaks in the moment Hassan takes to return. When he is back, our eyes meet, and I doubt he forgot the keys. Perhaps Hassan has done what I did not.

We ride back through the city. It makes no sense, this whole day and the last night, this journey, if one may call it so. Somewhere along the road, Hassan has taken a detour, and we ride beside the lake. The mountains form an arc in shades of blue, their distant tops glistening in the sun. It is quiet and still, everything so beautiful, even the green scum on the lake. It feels like a dream. Hassan still does not speak.

"ARE YOU SURE?" Hassan asks, dropping me near the Taxi Stand. "Why don't you take the bike and I will walk home?"

There is no grudge in his eyes, but a distance, a tired blankness. I would like to walk for a while, I say.

"Don't stay out too long," he says.

I know, I say.

"I will see you, then," he says. "And one of these days if you are free come home for lunch. Mother will be happy to see you."

Of course, I say. I would love to see her and everyone else.

He rides away slowly, giving me time to reconsider, and I do, till he turns and disappears into the bend, leaving behind a sudden silence.

I see the soldiers from a distance. They were watching me even before, and as I walk closer, I regret not simply riding home with Hassan. Nothing will happen, I tell myself. Do not look at them. Just walk past. This is your home. I hear their voices. "Aaaeeeeiiiii . . ." a soldier shouts. I want to hold on to something. With his index finger another calls to me. Broken lines pass through my head, but I am unable to hold on. There are six of them, but with their camouflage jackets and helmets and guns they look like an army. I pull out my wallet to show my card. "Put it back," one of them says. I put it back.

"Take off your shoes." For a moment I remain silent, looking at him. "Take them off," he says again. Why? I look him in the eyes and the soldier's boy eyes falter under the visor of his helmet. "Take them off, bastard," another shouts over my shoulder. Their hands tighten about their guns, they close in around me. Someone grabs at my collar, cold knuckles against my neck. "Sit down." I sit. They seem about to hit me, and with my hand raised above my head I wait for the blow. Between hitting me and not hitting me stands nothing, except their whim. Hunched on my toes, I unlace the shoes. "Will your mother take them off for you?" I take off the shoes, pull down my socks. No longer a poet, no longer a teacher, no longer anything, I am just a man stripping barefoot. The soldier kicks away my shoes; the socks lie limp on the pavement. "Walk now," one of them says. "Walk," they shout.

My feet against the pebbles, I walk on the uneven road. In a language unknown to me one of them says something; laughter rises behind me. I feel robbed. Gravel pares at my soles. I must hold back the tears. Avoiding the pebbles, avoiding the puddles, avoiding the bitter smoke welling in my eyes, I walk, till my foot lands in a crater filled to the brim with dirty water. The froth sticks to my foot, rising halfway up my calf. I turn back to the soldiers, to make them see my face, and to see in their faces if I might now return to my life. "Walk, bastard." One of them raises his rifle. "Walk." The bottom of my trouser glued to my leg, and dust and grit gathering against my soles, I walk on the broken deserted road. This road that I have walked a thousand times, and a thousand times more in my absence, I do not recognize it. It is a different road, one I see for the first time, a road ripped out from a road. Far away in the window of a house are silhouettes of a man and a child. They have been watching all along, and the way they look, their eyes unblinking, they seem to have seen it before. Gradually their faces obscure behind the glass. The child waves softly at me, or maybe he just rubs the vapor away. We look at each other till a wall blocks my view of them. A shadow leans on this wall, flits beside me, half on the road, half on the bricks. From far behind the soldiers shout. Motherfucker. Take back your shoes. Broken at the waist, the shadow drifts past other shadows. Stop. Shoot this bastard. Branches of trees sway in the dust, birds fly in dirty puddles, my feet walk on their own, and beside me a dark mass moves in its own quiet way.

Beauty

NONE OF US KNEW HER REAL NAME. WE HEARD HER MOTHER call her Beauty and she became Beauty for all of us.

The day she arrived we were in the yard of Jana's house, waiting desperately for the rain. Sameer had been hitting the ball all over the large yard, and nothing we did, chucking, distracting, changing the ball, nothing could get him out that afternoon. Our hopes clung to the gray clouds taking over the sky, threatening to wash away everything. And when we saw from a distance a thin-mustached man open the tin gate and a long, beaten-up vehicle drive in, we immediately knew that they were the tenants Jana had told us about.

"They have a daughter too," he had said. "And you know what? She is our age."

The driver was the first to climb down, and he and the mustached man, who we understood to be the father, looked briefly toward the sky and then hurried to remove the green tarpaulin that covered the back of the vehicle. The rear door opened and a plump woman got down, holding a stuffed handbag against her chest like a baby, and behind her came the girl, and she held nothing in her hands.

"To fall in love with Brother," Jana whispered beside us, "here she comes."

Jana always referred to himself as Brother. He would enter the classroom and before even taking off his backpack he would stand in front of us: "Yesterday Brother killed a girl with his gaze," and he would look at us with an intense, almost angry stare. "And guess what? She gave Brother a flying kiss! Oh, Brother almost died."

Now he was running toward the tenants and we watched him run, his silky black hair rising and falling, and ahead of him the girl. But she looked nothing like we had pictured her from Jana's stories.

He had told us of her dance at a distant cousin's wedding in the village. "It was the best dance ever," he had said, "until Brother break-danced and everyone had their jaws dropping."

In Jana's stories she had long blond hair. In reality, though her hair was long, it was not blond but black, and she wasn't white like snow. For a moment I thought another girl was going to step out of the vehicle: milky white, blond, each breast the size of Raju's head. Hadn't we long known, though, that Jana's stories were made up of more lies than truths, and yet we loved to listen to him, and we believed him too, because no one told a story the way Jana did, not merely with words but with his arms and legs, and his eyes, punctuating those long tales with whistles and sighs, and with music from his mouth, which he called the beat-box. When he had told us of her dance, we saw her whirl in the middle of a small gathering, her arms outstretched and her yellow and gold dress billowing in the air, blond hair turning round and round, one slash enough to take you out for life. By popular request the two of them had danced together, and all along while they swayed to the music, their eyes had been talking. He even did a little jig, showing us his arm wave and rope walk from that night, and then her moves too, all hips and ass. What Jana had strangely forgotten to tell us, though, and what struck me the most from the distance, was how tall she was. She was taller than her parents, and when Jana, who was taller than me, hugged her father and then her mother, she was clearly taller than him too. The rain that had hung in the air for so long broke into our faces and our eyes and I suddenly felt weaker in my legs.

"Don't look at her like that," Waheed said. "It will go to her head."

Raju said he wasn't looking at her.

"You must be looking at her mustached father then," Waheed answered.

"No, you are looking at the father," Raju shot back. "Because your father, too, has a mustache."

Sameer said we should help them before the rain ruined their stuff.

"Let them call us and we will go," Waheed said. "We shouldn't go on our own. These village girls, they climb on your head if you give them a little lift. What does Jana know, rushing like that? Fool!"

From beneath the giant pear tree we watched Jana's mother and grandmother and his aunt come out of the house, and one after the other embrace the mother and the girl. Jana's mother held her for so long that we thought she might never release her. "That is how I would like to embrace her," Raju whispered beside me. And when Jana's frail little grandmother shouted at us, calling us shameless for watching the guests work, all of us ran through the rain, except Waheed who walked slowly, looking down at his bright red and white shoes and brushing with his fingertips his meticulous hair. I wanted to fall back with him and walk at my own pace, but I kept running behind Sameer and Raju.

THE SACKS WERE KNOTTED out of bedsheets, curtains, dupattas, and we carried them from the bed of the vehicle to one of the rooms upstairs. My sack held clothes and Raju's held pots and pans, and he kept saying that his load was heavier than mine. By the time we carried the second load, our wet shirts were stuck to our bodies, but none of us seemed to mind. Raju stopped me on the stairs and asked in a whisper if I had seen the mole on the girl's chest. I hadn't, I said. "Women with a mole on their chest," he said, "want to be in bed all day." I tried to remember if any of the women I knew had a mole on their chest, but it seemed I had paid no attention to moles. So while her father passed Raju and me the heavy, worn-out leather suitcase tied together with a rope, I stole glances at the girl's chest. It was a small mole, a little bigger than a dot, but it wasn't on her chest but on her left collarbone. And when I said this to Raju on the stairs, he looked at me and said that anything below the throat on a woman was chest. While we waited to be handed another sack, I kept stealing glances at that mole on her chest, till she turned her head to look at Jana's aunt and there, just beside her earlobe, I glimpsed yet another dark dot. I had seen moles for the first time.

The girl was not our age. That was clear. And even if she was, there was something older about her that was different from the girls in our class, even the girls in the classes above us. She was there and not there at the same time, and even though her gaze passed over us several times, she did not seem to see any of us.

The luggage ended quickly and we looked with disappointment at the empty soaked bed of the vehicle. Jana climbed onto it to see if anything had been left behind even though it was clear that nothing had been left behind. A very light rain kept falling and the girl's mother stood with Jana's mother on the veranda. She was crying, the girl's mother, and when I walked a little closer, I heard Jana's mother say that God was kind and merciful and that she should think of this home as her home too. Then they started whispering the way my mother and aunts sometimes did at home, and while they whispered, Jana's mother was looking at the girl in a slanting way. I walked a step closer. I still could not hear them, and just as I took another step, both of them turned toward me at the same time. A thief who had been caught, I limped away, pretending that something was pinching my foot. The girl stood with Jana's aunt under the awning of a window. Jana lingered near them now. I looked at her face and her lips and those clear big eyes that seemed not to rest on anything. Jana winked at me, a signal to come over, and I thought about it but the image that came to me was of not even coming up to her shoulder. The mere thought diminished me. Waheed, Sameer, and Jana would have some chance with her or at least they could stand beside her without embarrassment; even Raju, who wasn't much taller than me, would be beside her soon because he didn't care, he didn't care at all how short or tall or dumb he was. But I did, and the only exchange I could see between the girl and me was shame. And yet, along with everyone I hated Jana for being the only one who would spend the evening around her, as she would gradually settle down and speak, and smile, and stretch her legs, and maybe dance too. When he saw the envy in our eyes, Jana's happiness doubled.

"Beauty," her mother called, looking toward her. "Get the radio from the vehicle."

With gentle steps she walked on the wet pathway and, leaning into the window, brought the radio out, a black radio in a leather cover with the familiar circle of pinpricks. We had the same one at home and almost everyone I knew had one in theirs, and yet in her hands the radio looked like a new thing, a thing of magic, come from some other world. Its handle loose in her fingers, she passed me by and not once did she look at me. Through the hurriedly fallen evening we watched her disappear into the house, and though we should all have been home by now, we remained on quietly in the fine rain. I knew more than anyone what awaited me at home: every passing minute harshening the inevitable beating that was my fate, and yet that fate seemed so distant from me and so insignificant.

EVERY MORNING JANA came to school with stories of Beauty. We gathered around him, holding on to his every word. She had asked for his help to fasten a rope across the veranda, and he had then stood there talking to her and watching her hang the clothes on the clothesline, and she had smiled and blushed when, after all the others, she placed on the rope her lingerie. "What color?" Raju asked even before Jana had finished. "Black," Jana said. "Black," all of us whispered. The next day Jana said Beauty's leg had gone to sleep while they were watching TV, and with his arm around her waist she had hopped the long corridor of their house. "At her waist," Jana said. "Brother touched the most tender flesh in the whole universe." He kissed the fingers of his right hand, and we grabbed at his hand and ran it over our faces, giggling, playacting, but also hoping for his fortune to touch us.

Of the four of us I had the greatest appetite for Jana's stories. I wanted them to never end, and sometimes, when Jana and I were on our own, walking around at the lunch hour, or sneaking out on pee breaks at the same time, I asked him to tell a story again. Jana always did, with slight changes here and there, and at times I even reminded him of something interesting he had forgotten. It made me feel part of the story, made me feel closer to Beauty. I had, after all, not seen her since that first time. After a long whipping at home that evening for returning late, I was forbidden to go out to play from the next day on. It was the most terrible punishment and it had come at the worst time, when my heart was in Jana's yard, where all the afternoon games had moved. Even Waheed had stopped caring about his video games. I promised at home that I would never return late again, I swore that we had a tournament going on at Jana's house, that I had contributed three rupees to this tournament, but my family said that I could no longer go out. Going out to play was a privilege, my father said, one that I didn't deserve. So while Jana, Raju, Waheed, and Sameer were having the time of their lives with Beauty, I was imprisoned in the empty garden of our home. I aimed pebbles at the small thorny chestnuts in the large chestnut tree, and I kicked and swiped at the tall grasses and the dandelions, the sight of whose destruction gave me pleasure, and I hurled the tennis ball into the air, hoping for it to rise far into the sky, and watched it turn back and fall as if hitting some invisible ceiling. Sometimes I forgot about the punishment, about the source of my sadness, sharing vacantly in the quiet stillness of everything in the garden—the fruits, the flowers, the birds, the grass, the frogs hopping around, the butterflies—only for the question to suddenly and piercingly stab into me: What must be happening at Jana's home at that very moment?

At school, I urged Jana for more stories even though Waheed and Sameer kept saying that they were not true and I knew as well that a lot of them were Jana's fantasies, but what fantasies: an insect flying into Beauty's right eye at dusk and no one around except Jana and how gently he had wet in his mouth the tip of his finger and taken his time to draw that dark little unknown insect out from the pink underfold of her lower eyelid. How many times later at home, looking over my books, or lying sleepless in the nights, did I imagine myself in Jana's place: Beauty's face in my hands, all the time in the world in my hands? How many dark unknown insects did I remove from the underfold of her eye, how many variations of the same moment did I invent and live, how many possibilities did that one moment open, what unknown paths it led through my heart?

I started spending more time staring into the oval mirror in the bathroom, observing myself under the very bright light that illuminated it. Nothing of that face that looked back from the glass consoled me. A dark face with curly side-whiskers, the shameful fuzzy beginnings of a mustache, hideous gap teeth, and short rough hair; it was a mess and I washed it again and again in hope and in despair. All that was ugly had been thrown my way and there seemed to be nothing I could do except dream with my eyes open. And in my dreams I was as tall as Beauty, sometimes even taller, my skin without a single blemish, and I smiled when she ran her fingers through my smooth long hair, and I told her all about myself. The punishments, the beatings, the urge to run away and never return, the desire to go to a big city where the lights never dimmed, where there were no clocks to tell time. She too had dreamt of a city, not this one, another; it might even be, she said, that both of us had been dreaming the same city. We held each other close, for so long that sometimes I fell asleep in her embrace, an embrace in which I dissolved into the warm softness of her body, only to be woken up by the yelling of my family, demanding that I wake from slumber or calling me to eat or cursing me for having forgotten something yet again.

After five long days of imprisonment, I was again allowed to go out; "but if you don't return in an hour and a half," my father said, "we will come to Jana's home and beat you so bad that you will be ashamed to ever go there again." They said other things too that I barely heard because I was already halfway to Jana's in my head. I oiled my short curly hair, put on a different shirt, wiped at my shoes with a rag. On the street a strong breeze blew, and my shirt flapped against my body, making me wish for my hair to be longer, for Beauty to see me with the breeze caressing it.

I saw them the moment I opened the gate. They were on the veranda. Beauty was sitting on a chair and Jana's aunt sat on the armrest, and Jana, Sameer, Waheed, and Raju stood on the other side of the veranda's iron railings. I had the feeling I was walking all wrong. They were looking toward me and saying something and smiling at the same time, and, my feet sinking into the earth, I saw myself as I must have appeared to them. I wanted to turn and run back into my prison, but I kept on walking with my head down. "How did Mummy let you come, littley?" I heard Waheed's voice. "Did you cry at home?" Raju said. They laughed. I tried to smile. "His mummy's sent him in a new shirt," Jana said. "Doesn't he look dashing?" Even his aunt laughed.

Beauty was looking toward me, but she was not laughing. When I got to the veranda I didn't know how to stand, where to keep my arms, whom to look at. "You look good with your face oiled," Jana said. "Stop it," Jana's aunt said, laughter in her voice. "He looks very good." That embarrassed me more than everything. She asked about my aunt and told Beauty that my aunt used to be in her class but our family got her married and now she had a child already. "Is she happy?" Jana's aunt asked me. "I don't know," I said. "Why? Is she not your aunt?" My aunt had forbidden me from saying anything to Jana's aunt. "To every question she asks about me," my aunt had told me the first time she came home crying from her in-laws', "just say that you don't know." "Tell," Jana's aunt said. "How is she? Has she put on weight? Does she still wear lipstick? Is she expecting?" I said nothing and looked down, and there, one crossed over the other, I met Beauty's feet, long and arched, her toes thin and long. "She is a lot of fun," Jana's aunt told Beauty. "Or has she become boring after marriage?" I went on looking at Beauty's feet, at the toes and the nails, at the few hairs on her foot, and when I looked up she was looking at me as if she knew what I was hiding and I noticed another dark speck at the corner of her eyelid. Amid all the talking and the laughter she again seemed to be somewhere else. Once or twice her eyes rested on me and before I knew it, my time was over.

That night I lay beside her in the vast darkness under the quilt, and I traced with my finger the dark scatter of moles on her skin. At each new discovery my eyes glimmered in surprise. Beside her ankle I found a little fleck and two dots that hid unseen in the back of her knee; there they were, sprinkled at her waist, and deep between her breasts, and along her throat, at the corner of her lips, at the edge of the eyelid, a great constellation coming together.

Every day we gathered in the yard around Jana's house, playing listlessly and distractedly, hoping for Beauty to come out, devising schemes to make her join us. Sometimes she came to the window and I tried to smile at her up there but she wasn't looking at me or at any of us, even though Jana kept insisting that she came to the window for him. One day Jana said he had figured out the problem. "Fools, we have been fools." He pulled the stumps out from the pitch. "How could Brother be so blind, asking her to join us at cricket?" He threw the wickets behind the evergreen bushes and tossed the bat on top of them. "Badminton," he said. "Badminton is what girls play." A bulb had suddenly lit up in great darkness, and everyone agreed, and while we tied the tattered old net we told Jana that he must call her when she came to the window. And he did.

"Come, come," Jana said, "you will beat us all." She looked at him and gestured no with her head. He stood beneath the window while the rest of us looked up from farther away. She stood there quietly for a while, almost smiling behind the glass, and then she went away, leaving the window empty, plunging everything into darkness again. "She is coming down," Jana announced, rubbing together his palms and snatching the racket from Raju's hand. "Didn't Brother say badminton is the trick?" Raju was so happy at her coming that he didn't even fight for the racket. But I knew that she was not coming, and she did not come, and I no longer felt like playing and no one else wanted to play either.

Our old routines had been smashed to pieces, our old pleasures were no longer ours; what was ours now was the distractedness and impatience and the boredom. Waheed and Sameer were upset that we just lay around listening to Jana's farts, which was what, between themselves, they called his stories, and soon they started coming late and leaving early and then they stopped coming altogether. Raju said they now played video games at Waheed's home. "We should go check," he said. He, too, was tired of sitting under that giant tree that bore small worm-eaten pears, but Jana said Sameer and Waheed could go fuck themselves and play cartoons like children. "We are men," he said. "We will do love."

ONE AFTERNOON AT SCHOOL, during the lunch break, Jana took me aside. His arm around my shoulder, we walked to the far end that housed the primary classes. Children came slipping down the metal slide, went back and forth on the swings, and turned on the creaking merry-go-round. "Hold on tight," Jana shouted, grabbing at the bar of the merry-go-round, and he ran, spinning the wheel faster and faster, and the children clenched their hands tighter around the bar. We hopped on next to each other. Jana looked at me in a silence that wasn't usual to him.

"What?" I asked.

"Do you want to see her naked?" Jana said.

We rose a little and dipped back again. The children yelled around us.

He said he had seen her bathing in the small bathroom, through the gap between the floor and the base of the door.

"Did you, really?" I asked.

"Does Brother ever lie!" he replied.

"What did you see?"

"What do you think?"

He had seen water dripping down her calves and her ankles, and her feet were moving around in their small bathroom, and when he had gone closer to the gap, he had seen what she was doing inside. Dancing. Naked. Her legs moving, her arms swaying, her breasts bigger than they looked in the clothes. "Just as I had told you," he said.

"Was she also singing?" I asked.

"Listen to me," Jana said, the seriousness returning to his face. "I know you also love her. Don't lie to me. I know everything."

"I do," I said.

"I know. Which is why I am asking you."

The wheel was screeching to a halt and Jana jumped off. "Hold on tight," he shouted again, pushing at the bar, raising plumes of dust with his feet, and the children, their eyes widening, kept saying, "Faster, faster, faster."

Jana climbed back on, but he said nothing. I would rather have heard him tell the story, even if the whole thing was nothing but lies, but he was looking at me, asking with his eyes if I was up to it. "Yes," I said.

"But we can't tell the others. It must be our secret."

"Why not?" I asked. "I think Raju would want to come."

"Raju can't hold his tongue," Jana replied. "He will tell everything if they give him a shot at the video game."

"But Waheed and Sameer too might want to see. Don't you think so?"

"They are good boys." Jana winked at me. "They want to go to heaven. Let them go."

I knew Waheed and Sameer would have said no. They would also have tried to wean us away, telling us that it was a sin, that God would throw us into hell.

"What if we get caught?" I asked.

"We won't," he replied. "Brother has a foolproof plan. Tomorrow afternoon; the best Sunday of our life."

That night I dreamt of Beauty for the first time. It was a strange dream. We were all looking for mushrooms at the edge of Jana's yard. My aunt was there too, cradling a baby, and Jana's aunt kept telling her that it was a doll and not a baby, and it was, indeed, a doll with a plastic face, but it was also somehow my aunt's baby. We found big mushrooms, their heads large as saucers that fell down as soon as we held them in our hands. At some point Beauty's leg went to sleep, and I ran to help her, but my own legs suddenly wouldn't move. And the harder I tried, the more my legs were stuck, and I started to yell in panic, but I couldn't even cry, and then everyone laughed, Jana, Waheed, Sameer, Raju, but we were no longer in Jana's yard but in an abandoned house whose windows were covered with yellow plastic sheets and the floor strewn with hundreds of mangled slippers and shoes.

JANA WAS WAITING for me at the gate, agitated, cracking his knuckles again. "What took you so long?" he asked. I said I got held up at home. "Ten more minutes and the show would have been over." I did not reply. Then Jana looked at me and asked if I wanted to do it or had I, too, become a saint. "Why would I come otherwise?" I replied.

It was dark in the corridor, and our eyes took time to see in that darkness. Only his grandmother was home and Jana went to check on her, and when he returned he said everything was fine: sleeping like a corpse. He had locked her door from outside, and if she knocked, he would say it must have been a mistake. "Brother's plan, foolproof." His lips pulled into a smile, but he looked nervous, the same way he did on the morning of exams. We stood outside the brown bathroom door, hearing the rustle of the water as it fell from the tap into the bucket. My heart began to pace. What if someone walked in from the outside or Beauty opened the door suddenly, what would we do then, and once it reached my family, what would happen to me?

Jana went down first, prostrating, his head turned to the side. I followed him. The concrete of the floor cold against my face, I heard my heart thump. Through the thin bright gap between the floor and the base of the door I saw the drifting fog, white and translucent, in which I made out the color of skin, but nothing clear till I adjusted my head and my eyes, and then I saw her, amid the mist of that steam, sitting on a low wooden seat, naked and curved forward, her calves drawn tight against her, water falling. But I could only see till her waist, so I crawled ahead, leaving behind Jana, who had been ahead of me all this while. Her wet hair stuck to her shoulders like a dark rich cloth; vapor rose from her left breast. I pressed against the concrete to see her face, I shuffled ahead a few more inches, my own face now barely away from the door. I no longer seemed to care that someone might come and find us. All I wanted was to see her face, and for some reason her hands remained glued to her face. I kept looking, waiting, till she finally lifted them. She looked strange, her face almost warped in the mist, her face a mask, as if she were someone else. I knew it was her, though. Jug after jug of hot water she poured over her head, the haze thickening around her; she blew her nose, poured more water over her head and snorted her nose again, and then holding her face low in her hands she remained like that, shaking, uttering again and again, "What had I done to you, my God? What had I done to you?"

I turned to look at Jana, who at that same moment with stunned eyes looked at me. I ran past him through the dark corridor, past the latched door, past the yard, and stumbling over rotting fruit, past the pear tree, and ran and ran through the mist that blurred away everything.

Flowers from a Dog

EVERY EVENING I HAD PROMISED MYSELF NEVER TO RETURN to this city, our city, and after years of promises, here I was, searching for her, carrying under the folds of my jacket the handful of flowers I had picked along the way.

All through the journey, on the flights and in the waiting areas, I had imagined this moment a thousand times, but always thought this graveyard would be small, like the one where many years ago my grandmother and then grandfather were buried and where, before them, my father had lain in a corner forever. I had, in fact, seen it as the same square graveyard fenced by low brick walls, and I hadn't thought I would have to search for her. I had seen her all along at the center, as if all the dead in their graves had made way for her. How foolish it had been of me to imagine her like that, dignified and distinguished in death, exacting a special treatment.

The graveyard spread out in vast brightness. Afraid all along of running into someone here, now I looked around for help, and it offended me that amid all these dead that meant nothing to me, my love could not guide me, that I was looking for her now in these rows, mechanically, as one looked for things.

Row after row, no trace of her among all the names engraved on the stones. No sign anywhere. The sun climbed higher, not one leaf fluttered on the trees. I walked on with the flowers in my hand.

She loved white roses. We had grown them tall in the narrow flower bed that ran along the wall of our small home. How she looked at them, lingering over each one, telling me that if I really looked, I would see that no two were the same. How many times had I seen her bring her face close to the flowers, with her eyes closed, that wart alive on the corner of her eyelid?

And for years, after she was gone, I smelled all the white roses in all the gardens and vases, and all of them smelled of her. Now here she was, in a place where the dead lay in little families: husbands, wives, children, huddled together, some even enclosed by iron fences. It suddenly occurred to me that I had yet to read a woman's name on the stones. All along, while I had been looking for her name, I should have been searching for her husband's name. I feared I might have walked past her already, left her behind in one of the rows, and if it was true, that I had trodden over her and felt nothing, then what was all that love and hurt that I had proclaimed for years? Was she right, then, that I went around seeking pity, that in love with my misfortune, I was afraid to live without my halo of victim and martyr?

I walked slowly, reading the names out loud, looking around for water, beginning to feel lost in the sound of my own strange voice. My shadow dragged beside me like a small dark animal. I had arrived here clear in my mind and now I walked on in a parched daze, the bright expanse ahead of me growing bigger.

Had the whole city died? Was there no one here to show anyone around? It would take hours to walk all these rows and even then I might not find her. Maybe I had really left her behind.

I murmured her name, again and again, the way years ago she had read the ninety-nine names of God on those green beads that shone through the nights. What did she seek through those nights, counting away the darkness? She must have found what she wanted or she wouldn't have left those beads behind when she departed for her new home.

I stopped in the slight shade of a willow tree, looking around for some sign of water. In the distance were old brick houses, their tin roofs glinting in the midday sun. The air quivered in the heat. A young man's grave lay near my feet, its white stone almost fallen over. Born in '73, killed in the spring of '96, he had been younger than me when he died, by seven years. Was I ready to die? But maybe he wasn't ready either. Maybe no one was ready to die. What would be left of him down there now? Did the skin disappear in twenty years, what happened to eyes, to teeth, to hair, when did the bones start to give way? Whoever he was, he must have been someone. Did anyone even think of him now? Not far from this grave, purple irises glimmered under the noon sun. I wondered if the same flowers grew by her grave. The roses I had brought were misshapen already and limp. I should have brought something with roots instead, something that wouldn't die in hours. Even this had turned out to be a mistake. I had come to sit by her grave, not to complain, not to offer apologies, but to meet her in silence, and here I was, already reduced to tears. Some cruel hand had pulled out the years from behind me and abandoned me again into a child. I knew I should calm down and look for water and find someone to guide me through this dead city. I wasn't a boy anymore. That was over, an entire life stood in between.

A MAN'S VOICE startled me. I never saw him coming. We shook hands. He was the caretaker of the graveyard. His hand rough and callused, its solidity brought a strange moment of comfort, and I held it till he withdrew.

"Do you have someone buried here?" he asked.

"Yes, a relative. But I can't find her grave."

"Don't you know where she is buried? It is not a small graveyard."

"No," I said.

"When did she die?"

"Last week."

He said a few people had died over the last week, three of them women.

"They are buried at different places. One is over there." He stretched his arm above my shoulder, pointing far behind me. "And another there." He pointed toward where I had come from. "Where was she from?" he asked.

I told him the name of the place where our home had been.

"Are you sure?" he asked. "No one from there was buried here. It is too far from there."

I named the place then where she had lived after her marriage, her husband's home, her home, the home of their children, and his small old eyes immediately lit up, brightening his furrowed face.

"Are you looking for the grave of Sham Saeb's wife?" he asked.

"Yes," I said. "Her."

"Of course, she is buried here. This is their ancestral graveyard. Sham Saeb's parents are also buried here."

The old man started walking purposefully, and I followed him.

"Are you related to her?" he asked.

"Yes," I said. I went on walking behind him, looking in silence at the uneven land beneath, full of crevices and burrows, and at graves on the verge of collapsing.

"It is an odd day of lull here, otherwise you could always see someone being buried," he said. "War is a thousand plagues put together, picking the young, leaving the old to bury them."

We passed beneath two enormous chinar trees, large and lush, belonging to some other time. Who would have planted these trees? Held them, little saplings, in their hands and put them in small holes dug into the earth, watered them; someone must have, like we did that afternoon in our courtyard. Everyone told her that almond trees grew big and our yard was small, but she said every home needed a tree, and what better than almonds? The small tree lay on her palm as I slashed with a blade at the black plastic bag that held its roots, and when we pulled off the bag, a little earthworm had been torn into two. "They will both live," she said. "Now there will be two of them."

"Where do you live?" the old man asked. The way he looked at me I felt he had asked me the question before and I hadn't heard.

"In Riyadh," I said. "Saudi Arab."

"Subhan Allah, the holy land."

I nodded.

"Have you performed the pilgrimage?" he asked.

"No."

"You should visit while you are young," he said. "Worship in youth pleases God. At my age, what is left to do except prayers? And what is it but kneading water."

We walked for a while in silence. I hoped for it to last.

"Do you work there?" he asked.

"Yes."

"What kind of work?"

"Construction. In the desert."

"May God give you success. All of Sham Saeb's family is well educated and at big positions, in all the countries. His parents were heavenly people, may God bestow his grace upon them. I buried them with my own hands many years ago. He turned to look at me again. "Are you related to her from Sham Saeb's side?"

"No," I said.

"From her parents' side, then?"

"Yes." The rows seemed to stretch on and on. "How far is it?" I asked.

"Not far. Are you tired?"

"No."

I followed him, listening to the sound his cracked heels made each time they met the moist discolored hollows of his rubber sandals.

"Everyone has to go under the earth one day," he suddenly said. "That is the truth. These houses, like palaces, what use? From him we come, and unto him we return. The body is a mere feast for the worms."

The moment he mentioned the worms, I saw them. Maggots, swarms of them, like I had seen one evening on a dog rotting away by the banks of the river, her mouth covered by thousands of the same teeming little white worms. I tried to wipe away the image, but it stuck. I felt loathing for the old man for destroying with his maggots my memory of her.

"What is man?" he said. "Born from clots of blood. Mud. Dust."

She was not dust. She was not mud. She was beautiful and full of love and she left me behind with a million maggots in my heart to go away with that engineer from a respectable family with relatives all across the world. She left, never to return, even though she loved me. How could she leave me behind? Why didn't she insist that I was a part of her, and that she couldn't part with me? I would have died for her and she couldn't even fight to make a little space for me in her new life. How could she not see that my life without her was nothing, that without her not just my body but my soul, too, was a feast for the worms. That man, what did he give her? A big house with lots of windows, a garden full of roses, a brighter life, two decent well-behaved children? And she went for it, returning occasionally, in beautiful dresses that she never had when she lived with us, returning with leftovers of love and guilty tears, and promises that she would soon take me with her, that she was making arrangements, and asking me to be gentle and good, and not to trouble anyone. She brought along packets of their rich food, cakes sometimes and ice creams that had always melted by the time she arrived, and money too, but not much, afraid that I might spoil myself. I didn't need their money to spoil myself; I did it on my own. How could she expect me to be well-mannered and gentle? Where would I have brought all that from when her love and absence rotted me away, convinced me that I was unrequired, unnecessary, worthless, left behind with old, wrinkled, decrepit people, a teenage dog with wounds that no fingers, except hers, could reach.

IT WAS A DAMP mound of earth, in the middle of a row, in the middle of the graveyard, with the sun right above. This woman whose shadows I had chased for years, the flame of whose absence I had circled hopelessly, here she lay, extinguished, so far away from the shade of any tree.

"Are you sure this is her grave?"

"You can read, can't you?" the old man said, his pride wounded in his voice.

I had not wanted to read that stone, afraid of what might be written on it, afraid of what wouldn't be on it. But there she was, wife of her husband, mother to her two children, dead a week ago, the little flowers along the borders leaving no space on the plaque for another name.

"They will soon make a marble tomb over her grave," he said. "One has to be careful of the dogs for the first few days. They smell the new dead and they claw at the earth. Filthy creatures."

I saw the traces where the dog had tried to dig with its small claws, and I felt this intense urge to put my fingers there and to dig and dig until I reached all the way down. I wanted to hold her one last time, to embrace her with all those worms. She couldn't go, she couldn't leave like that, she had to come back to me, I had imagined it a million times, that was why I had suffered and degraded and ruined myself, only for her to tell me some day that it had been a mistake, that she should never have left me behind, that without her I would eat away every little inch of myself.

The old man never left, his shadow leaning across the grave the entire time. And I sat beside him when all I wanted to do was to throw myself down at her grave, and wipe away all the names of gods and men from that stone. He raised his hands and prayed for her, for her grave to become vast, for God to be merciful to her, for her to be raised with the faithful on the Day of Judgment. Not far from where the dog had tried to dig, I left the flowers.

The House

JUST AS THEY WERE GATHERING NEAR THE MULBERRY tree for the afternoon tea, Manzoor, the new laborer digging at the house site, screamed God and came running through the narrow trenches with a spade in his hands. In two days of work, the head mason, ObduRahim, already knew Manzoor to be a talker and a work shirker, a white earphone always dangling near his ears. So, seated on a brick, ObduRahim went on pouring himself a cup of tea and watched Manzoor struggle out of the trenches that the next morning were to be filled with rocks and small boulders.

Covered in dark sticky earth, thin grimy finger bones lay limp on the end of the spade, and just above was a tattered rag that might once have been a palm.

"Where did you find this?" ObduRahim coughed up, the tip of his tongue burning with the first little sip of tea.

"There, where I was digging," Manzoor yelled, as if the head mason were far away.

ObduRahim looked at it, and the longer he looked, the less it appeared a hand, seeming from the left like a decayed knot of a tree's root, and from the right like some dead, muddy animal.

"Was it down there?" The other laborer walked close behind Manzoor and looked over his shoulder. Manzoor half turned and raised the spade for a better view. "Yes." The other laborer drew his lips into a close circle, sucked breath in, and with the index finger of his right hand, he marked down in the air an imaginary line. "It's been cut by a marble blade. Someone I know got his hand cut just like this, his arm hurt for a whole year. But this hand has been cut all the way off."

"Why does it have only four fingers, though?" Manzoor said. "Look. The little one is missing."

"The little finger is there." The head mason pointed with his finger. "It is the one before that is not there."

For a while they stood around it, looking and talking, till they saw, walking in through the large temporary tin gate, the owner of the house for which the foundation pit was being dug. The owner had just gotten off the phone with the architect, urging him to visit and see the digging one last time before the rockwork would begin in the morning. Behind him his wife followed with quick short steps, carrying in her hand the final design, in which the drawing room was bigger by twenty-eight square feet and the kitchen window was placed such that you only had to lift your head to see who walked in and out of the main gate. When the husband and wife were still a few steps away, Manzoor turned the spade toward them.

His head filled with the prices of rocks, iron, cement, bricks, and wood, MohmadYaesin, the owner, stared at the spade, at the four long spider legs emerging from the decayed lump. His wife covered her mouth and nose with the end of her scarf. Obdu-Rahim stood up, holding the cup of tea he had been looking forward to since lunch. When Yaesin finally understood what he was looking at, he lifted his eyes from the spade and looked at Manzoor.

The spade ahead of him, Manzoor jumped back into the narrow trenches. The others followed from the ground above, walking beside the heaps of extracted soil. The owner and his wife watched Manzoor carefully. His legs faltered on the slippery soil in the trench. The grimy white wire of his earphone jerked and swayed by his greasy collar at every step. This was the most energy he had shown since he had come to work here.

He turned at the bend in the trench where the walls of the kitchen were to be, and walked straight through the storage and laundry room, and then stopped. "Here," he said, looking around his feet. "Yes. Here it was."

The owner looked where Manzoor pointed with the spade. This was where the wall of the children's room was to be. There was nothing there except damp dark earth.

"Are you sure it was there?" he asked Manzoor.

"Of course. I was digging here." He pointed ahead of his feet. "I thought, Let me get out a few more spades and then have tea, and there it came. I thought at first it was a scorpion or some such monster. But then I saw."

Their bodies blocking the afternoon sun that would otherwise have fallen on Manzoor's narrow, clean-shaven face, they looked around even though no one was sure what they were looking for. The owner stared vacantly into the damp soil.

"This is an animal's doing," the owner's wife suddenly said. "Isn't the graveyard five minutes away?" She raised in her hand the rolled-up design and pointed with it toward the tall brick wall, behind which was the house of the zonal officer who, too, it seemed, had had his eye on this plot and was morose that someone else had clinched it. Behind his house was another house, and then another, house after house after house, some new, some decaying, and others in various stages of construction and reconstruction, all of them standing haphazardly along narrow lanes that eventually found their way to the road. There, on the road, opposite the auto-rickshaw stand, was the graveyard. "A grave must have caved in," she said, "and a dog or some other animal has then disrespected the body and left it here. That is the problem with living near a graveyard."

No one looked at her. Only Manzoor responded, looking up from the trench, his hand shielding his eyes. "But how was it three feet under the earth? Wouldn't the dog have left it on the ground?"

She looked at Manzoor. His face a patchwork of light and dark, the hand concealing something sinister in his eyes. It was clear that he would love to while the day away running around with the spade, while they would still have to pay him in the evening. "How would I know?" she answered. "Maybe there was a hole here. Or maybe someone did find it lying around and buried it respectfully, till you found it. And please keep it somewhere on the side now, it is not a toy to be carried from here to there and there to here."

"What is that?" the other laborer shouted. "Over there?" His eyes shocked round, his mouth open, he pointed between Manzoor's feet, and Manzoor staggered back so quickly that the hand slid off the spade.

"Where?" Manzoor yelled.

"There."

Everyone looked near Manzoor's brown plastic shoes, searching in the shadow of his legs and in their own misshapen shadows that stretched far across the trench.

The head mason turned to the laborer. "Where?"

"There . . . I tho—I . . . in the shadow . . ." He lowered his head, the hint of an embarrassed smile hiding along his lips. They looked at him in silence, and he blushed under the sun. The wife mumbled under her breath, "One's house burns, another warms their hands." Manzoor slid the spade under the fallen hand and picked it back up. The owner touched the head mason's shoulder, and together they walked away beside the trench.

"WHAT SHOULD WE DO, ObduRahim?" MohmadYaesin asked.

"What can I say?" ObduRahim answered. He wanted to take a sip from the cup in his hand, but it seemed an odd thing to do at the moment, putting his lips to the rim of a cup and drinking. "You should seek someone's advice. Someone who knows." Two or three years older than Yaesin, ObduRahim, with a fistful of gray beard, could have passed for Yaesin's uncle. "Moulvi Yaqoob, perhaps," he said. "He knows religion, he knows the world, he may be able to guide you with this. But . . ."

"What?" MohmadYaesin asked.

With the toe of his rubber sandal ObduRahim fiddled with a dark round mulberry, rolling it over gently on the ground. MohmadYaesin watched the head mason's large, strange big toe. The mulberry turned the color of dust. "You know his wife," ObduRahim said. "She talks . . . and then you know people, they want something to talk about. Tomorrow if you want to . . . maybe . . . sell this place . . . for whatever reason . . . you know . . . one should think far. And even without that, you wouldn't want it getting around."

Yaesin had already thought of people talking when he stared into the trench. Even now he could hear the whispers, snatches of voices—his family, relatives, neighbors, colleagues at the office. He even heard Rahim's thick voice, telling his wife and children at dinner, telling in the mosque early in the morning, telling at the barbershop. People would form small pools in the neighborhood and count on fingertips his years of government service, and his salary, and calculate the price of the plot of land, they would come up with an amount for the house, too, and then talk as if no one among them had stuffed their pockets, no one taken money, as if he alone in this whole place was making a house and everyone else was clean, spotless, washed with milk. But the name that gets on the tongue gets on the tongue, the one who gets hit gets hit. The rest go home and eat dinner and talk about others.

"There was no need to go three feet deep, MohmadYaesin," ObduRahim said. "Didn't I tell you two feet of rockwork was more than enough? But you didn't listen. You were also right, though, you weren't saying anything wrong, God forbid. After all, you have gathered every penny for this house, you want it to be a fort, and why not, tied your belly and saved up the money, held back the hand and saved up money, slit the throat of a thousand desires. The whole neighborhood knows, gives your example. But I would have given you a fort at two feet."

His example. What example? ObduRahim had never mentioned it before. What else were they saying? A fort! Voices swirled in his head, buzzed in his ears, the sharpest among them the voice of his elder brother's wife. If this news reached her, she would go mad, she would stand on the roadside and stop every passing acquaintance and tell them, not that a hand had been found but that hands, feet, tongues, eyes, bodies upon bodies had been discovered beneath the earth of their plot, she would pay from her pocket to have it announced from the mosque loudspeaker. "Hello. Hello. One, two, three. One, two, three." A loudspeaker rang through his head. "Important notice. Important notice."

Yaesin shut his ears to the loudspeaker and turned to the head mason. "Should we tell the police, ObduRahim? I mean, if it is a hand . . . you know . . . and the word gets out somehow . . . the police might show up tomorrow and ask. What will we say then? I mean, we haven't done anything wrong. Why should we hide?"

ObduRahim looked at him. Furrows ran by the corners of Yaesin's lips, and even finer ones at the corners of his eyes. Not so young as he looked from a few feet away. "What can I say?" ObduRahim said. "You are an educated person, you know much more than I do. You must know many people. Officers. I am a poor mason. I stay away from them."

Yaesin, watching carefully the head mason's reaction, nodded in agreement. "Besides, it might be them," he murmured.

"Them yem hem," the mason replied. "If one digs too deep, MohmadYaesin, water and slush start coming out. Why descend there?"

He was right. Once they show up with their jeeps and boots and guns, who knew when and how they would leave, and wouldn't everyone get to know? It might come in the newspaper the next day, with his name, maybe even a picture of their tiny piece of land and, maybe, of this thing too. "We must bury it back," the owner said. "Respectfully."

"Yes," ObduRahim said. "That is the right thing to do."

"Yes. Best to do it quickly."

Now he felt he could take a sip, and quietly raising the cup to his lips, without making a sound, ObduRahim drank.

"But do you think it's the right thing to do, ObduRahim? I mean . . . you know . . ."

The tea had lukewarm, the salt was less, the milk watery. Obdu Rahim wanted to spit it out. "What can I say what is right?" he said, his mouth tasting queasy like those cough syrups. "I can at most tell what my mason's mind says. You are laying the foundation of your house. Going to spend forty, fifty lakh. On top of the land. It is no joke. But you shouldn't then, God forbid, carry things in your head, or pay attention to people's talks, or rumors, because somehow or the other word could get out. You yourself might tell someone, someone close to you, or your wife might, to her brother, maybe, or sister or anyone, or for that matter, even I, someday, perhaps by accident it could slip out of my mouth. A human being, after all, cannot be trusted until he is in the grave. If that is a big concern, then it is better to dig the whole thing up. But are we born yesterday, MohmadYaesin? You put a spade anywhere in this place too deep, from the north to the south, what might you find? Gold? Sapphire? Milk? Rest, you must decide. This is what my illiterate mind says. If I could think any better, I too would have been an officer, making my own house. Besides, you also have young children. That, too, you must keep in mind."

The children should have nothing to do with it. That Yaesin was clear about. They were too young. Ten and seven. It would frighten them, make them see shadows. They would fear going to the corner of the yard where his daughter was dreaming a swing, would be afraid even in their own room, running away from the little writing desks he dreamt of putting there. Forty, fifty lakh. ObduRahim had already dropped the number.

With steps slow and measured, and hands entwined behind her back, his wife walked toward them, taking her time beside the heaps of earth, her black flip-flops pressing down on the loose soil. "It is not a dog's doing," she said casually. "It is a bird. A bird has picked it up somewhere and then dropped it. This one must have been looking the other way. He anyway shuts his brains with plugs, wouldn't hear a bomb go off. Dead rats, pigeons, bones, fish heads, we are always picking up stuff cleaning the house. You wouldn't know. Any woman will tell you. It is the birds."

A bird dropping the hand from the sky, it seemed plausible, especially the way his wife said it, as if such things happened every day. He looked up at the washed blue sky. A few birds circled lazily amid distant gauzy clouds. A bird could pick it up somewhere and then drop it, and it would have to fall somewhere. It had fallen into the trench. It was possible. Why here, though, of all places, in their house? He breathed in a deep breath, a little of the emptiness of the vast blue sky seeping into his chest. The house felt distant, the land felt distant, he himself felt distant, and so too did the pictures he had torn out over three years, from newspapers and glossy magazines, of rooms, roofs, porches, possibilities of a garden in small spaces, and a solitary picture of a mezzanine with two armchairs and a round table that he knew he was never going to have, and yet he had kept it. He felt distant from the whole pile.

"Here," his wife was saying. "Here?"

Her dark small eyes shining under the thin arc of her neatly made eyebrows, she was looking at him. "Are you fine?" Pinheads of sweat glistened on her upper lip.

Yaesin gently nodded his head. "I am fine," he said. "We will bury it. That is what we were talking about. In the graveyard."

"Which graveyard?" she asked. "This?" She raised her arm toward the wall. "What if you run into someone there? Won't they ask what you are burying?"

"The auto drivers will be there," Yaesin said. "They will ask."

"We could bury it in that corner over there." ObduRahim pointed toward where they were planning to make a shed for wood and coal. "What came from there goes back in. And we could just move on with the day. As if nothing happened."

"No," the wife said. "Not here."

Yaesin looked at her, complaining with his face that she was making it more difficult.

"No," she reiterated. "Not in my home."

"Where then?" Yaesin asked.

"Anywhere. The world is so big. This city is so big. Rivers, lakes, mountains, garden after garden, garbage dump after garbage dump. Can you think of nowhere else but my house?" she said. "If there were ten kanals of land," she said, turning to the head mason, her eyes taking quick note of the cup in his hand, "or even two, one might have even thought about it, burying it somewhere and then forgetting altogether, but here, where it is already crammed with two and a half rooms, we will always be running into it. Am I saying anything wrong, ObduRahim?"

"No." The head mason nodded. "You are right."

"See, ObduRahim also agrees," she said to her husband, and asked him away with a quick movement of her eyes. ObduRahim, too, saw the gesture, and looked away. He asked if it was okay for him to go to the mosque to pray.

"Yes, of course," the owner said. "It is your own house, ObduRahim. You don't need to ask."

They watched him walk away, and when he did not turn to look back once, Yaesin wondered why he had suddenly decided to go to the mosque.

"What are you waiting for?" the wife said. "Why are you not getting rid of this thing? By now you should have been on your way back. That lunatic there is talking all kind of nonsense. Didn't I tell you only yesterday that he was no good, with these wires in his ears? Which laborer shaves their face every day, as if coming for a film shooting? He wants to run around the whole neighborhood with the spade in his hands."

From the corner of his eye the husband looked at Manzoor. Feet dangling in the trench, he sat on the ground, the handle of the spade resting on his thigh. "What was he saying?" Yaesin asked. The other laborer sat against the wall, smoking a cigarette, fiddling with his phone. The sight of the phone filled Yaesin with a sudden panic.

"Nonsense," the wife said. "See, he still isn't shutting that mouth. Blowing air into the other one, too. Was telling him some madness that lots of people vanished, and that bodies were never found. I wanted to slap him, but I walked away like I heard nothing. I hated him yesterday already. I told you. But you never listen to me."

"The problem is," the husband said, "that I listen to you. None of this would have happened had I not listened to you. 'Three feet down, three feet down . . .' Your brother has gone three feet down, now the whole world has to go three feet down. I told you let us finish at two, even two and a half I said, but no, your brother had gone three feet down. Now here we are, three feet in this plague."

"Bravo . . ." the wife said. "Bravo. Just when something goes wrong, turns out you listened to me. Well, had you listened to me, this lunatic would have not been here today. I won't be surprised if he brought this thing in his pocket."

"Why would he bring it in his pocket?" The husband clenched his teeth. "Dogs. Birds. Now pocket. Why?"

"How do I know why? I'm not inside his mind. But I am begging you now, please, for the sake of God, throw it away. Don't you understand? We have enemies. All around. Strangers, enemies, and our own even worse. If they only get a whiff, they will beat drums, they will take out a procession, they will shout from the loudspeaker. And if you can't do it, then get it from him and give it here, I will do it myself. Will go and throw it somewhere as if I am throwing away a dead rat. See, the lunatic is walking with the spade again. As if it will run away if he puts it down. If he talks any nonsense again, I swear on IfiJan's head I will slap him across that face."

"Don't you say anything," the husband said. "Let me handle it myself."

The earlier flush of energy no longer in his legs, Manzoor walked slower now. He looked tired. "Where did Master Rahim go?" he asked the owner.

"To pray," Yaesin replied. "Would you like to go?"

"No, no, I was just wondering where he went without telling us," Manzoor said. He looked down at his feet and then looked back up, at the owner. "What about this?" He turned to the spade. Neither husband nor wife looked at the spade. The owner looked Manzoor in the eyes and gently rested his hand on Manzoor's shoulder. "We are going to bury it in the graveyard, respectfully. ObduRahim also thinks the same. What do you think?"

"I think so too," Manzoor said. "After all, it is someone's hand."

"Yes. I am glad we all agree. Why don't you put the spade down, though? Your arms must be tired. Keep it to the side. Stretch your arms."

"I will," Manzoor said, "but . . . I was saying . . . shouldn't we, I mean . . . dig a little more? I mean . . . maybe, you know . . . it is not just the hand."

The wife let out a deep sigh. The husband clenched his teeth.

"I mean . . . we should dig, shouldn't we?"

"I am sure there is nothing in there," Yaesin said. "After all, we dug this whole thing up." He pointed at the trenches cutting into the earth. "If there was anything, would it have remained hidden till now? But, sure, for our own heart, we can look. But it is late right now, soon it will be evening. And it is not good to do such things around evening. We will do it tomorrow, first thing in the morning."

"It won't take long," Manzoor said, his face brightening again. "Majeed also thinks we should dig." He turned to the other laborer, who had taken off his shoes and set them beside him. "We will dig quickly. Two of us, half an hour, at most."

"But the tea is getting cold," the wife interjected. "It is a sin to waste food. A grave sin. First have tea and then you can go and dig. As if the land is going away somewhere. It will be here tomorrow morning as well. But the tea is getting cold. Come. Have tea first." She took a step toward the flask and the cups. "No bigger sin. Wasting food."

Manzoor stood there resolutely looking down at his feet. Just then the large temporary gate creaked open and the architect walked in with another man Yaesin and his wife had never seen before.

Beside the tall man the architect looked even shorter than he was, like a child walking with a father. The architect raised his hand from a distance, while the other man looked around, scanning the plot. The wife suddenly yanked the spade out of Manzoor's unknowing hands. He watched her hurry toward the mulberry tree and drop its contents behind it.

"Now please don't say I don't keep my promise," the architect shouted. With two quick spades of soil the wife covered the hand and then, after a moment's hesitation, turned another spadeful on top of it. "Sometimes one can get caught up, that is all," the architect said. "Where all can one reach, after all, on just two legs? How's the digging going? Seems you are finished."

"Thank God," Yaesin replied. "Almost done. Just stopped for tea."

"God sent you at just the right time," the wife said, walking back without the spade. "As if the tea was waiting for you."

The architect nodded a greeting toward her. "I got stuck at the bank director's house." He shook hands with Yaesin, giving his hand a firm squeeze with his small hand. "He has a big project going. Massive. If you see it, you might mistake it for a hotel. Italian marble from the main gate to the top floor. Only pine and walnut paneling. Imported windows. Heated floor even in the corridors."

The tall man looked at the trenches that ran all over in squares and rectangles of varying sizes, and at the black plastic water tank in the corner, and at the pale discolored hose that emerged out of it and snaked across the plot. The architect went on about the director's attic where five hundred people could sit for a feast at one time and yet one corner would remain empty. The tall man's gaze roved carefully and yet at the same time without interest, from the mulberry tree to the mound of sand, and leaping across the boundary wall to the neighbor's house.

Yaesin asked his wife to pour tea for the guests.

"No, no." The architect shook his head. "We just had juice at the director's house. I also have to leave quickly, there is another client whose house I am remodeling. Can't be everywhere at the same time. Just two legs, two arms. He, too, has been calling since yesterday. You must know of him. A big officer. I had done his colleague's house and since then he had been after me. You can't really say no to these people. I even quoted twice the amount to get rid of him. But he agreed to that too."

"Some people," the tall man said, "have magic pockets in their pants." He was looking at a bit of soil he had picked up from the heap. "They put their hand in the pocket and it meets money. They don't remember who put it there, nor do they care. You should have quoted four times more."

"He might have given that, too." The architect smiled. "But he is a good guy. You will see when we go there. Don't you miss his clothes, though. He could cut a watermelon by the crease of his pants."

Yaesin and his wife looked at them, the architect barely coming up to the tall man's chest, the two of them so different, and yet there was something similar about them. "Come, you have tea," the owner's wife said to Manzoor. He, too, was looking at the two men, and somehow he no longer looked sinister. "They only have almond tea and foreign juice, but you have to have our poor tea. Come."

"Please don't say that," the architect said. "I would gladly have had tea, I love tea, but there is no space left. How much can one stuff into a belly, after all?" He turned to the tall man. "You have some."

The man shook his head no. "Thank you," he said, "I don't drink tea."

"Who is this gentleman?" Yaesin asked the architect. "You haven't introduced him. Is he an architect too?"

"This gentleman." The architect turned to the tall man. "The less you know about him, the better. I know him for two years now, almost two and a half, and I swear by God I myself don't know him. Don't know what he actually does, don't know where he lives. Even his name, I swear, I have heard him called by at least a few."

The tall man smiled, only with the left side of his mouth, his lips too small and delicate for his face, as if they belonged to another face. "This man just wants to get me killed," he said. "That is why he introduces me like this even though I am a simple, straightforward, hardworking man. And he is my friend. But I have told him no matter what he does, I have been given in writing that I won't die till I am a hundred and two. So I let him do as he likes."

The couple looked at the man. "See," the architect said, "he didn't tell you his name still. Did he?"

A faint smile on his face, the tall man looked at the trenches.

"Who gave it to you in writing?" Manzoor suddenly spoke. He was looking up at the tall man, shielding his eyes with his hand even though the sun was now a fickle copper in a distant sky. "Except God who knows about life and death?"

The tall man looked at Manzoor, keenly. "What is your name?" he asked.

"Manzoor."

"Manzoor," the tall man repeated, pulling the name slowly out of his mouth like a long thread. "Manzoor Saeb," he said, "you are a good man. You have no business with these things."

"What things?" Manzoor asked. "I asked a simple question. Who here knows about life and death except God?"

"Money," the tall man said. "You have money, Manzoor Saeb, and you can find out too. Proper certificate. Sealed. Attested. As if from the DC's office. But as I said, you don't need to worry about these things."

"What has money to do with it?" Manzoor replied in a sharp voice. "Rich people die too. Don't they? Didn't Koroun die? AkbarBadshah die? HariSingh die?"

"See, this is what I tell you." The tall man turned to the architect. "ManzoorSaeb is a good person, but someday there might be someone crazy, and who can say what they might do? Might hit me with a spade, and just kick me in there. And will it be ManzoorSaeb's fault? No."

"But that will have to wait till you are a hundred and two," the architect said. "No? Poor ManzoorSaeb might not even be around."

Relieved at first by their arrival for saving them from Manzoor's insistence, the husband and wife could not wait for them to leave now. They hated the architect and hated this madman who somehow had no shame. The architect walked along the trenches, looking at the digging. Yaesin walked beside him. The wife followed. Manzoor stood there, stranded, waiting for the tall man to say something, but the tall man drifted away, too, but not toward the trenches.

"The stairs will go up from here," the architect said, "in a curve."

Barely listening to the architect, the couple watched the tall man's steps as he made his way toward the mulberry tree.

Reaching up with his left arm, he pulled low a high branch and, with other hand, plucked, one by one, berries, which he placed in his mouth.

"You, too, can make a fountain here," the architect said. "The director has put in a fountain. He will keep fish in it. Trout. Then you can someday invite us for dinner."

The tall man went on plucking berries, putting some in his mouth, some in the front pocket of his blue shirt.

"One of your neighbors," the architect said, "making money. Bought a big plot near the highway. He thinks no one knows. You know who. Don't you? The one expanding like a balloon. And sitting in the first row in the mosque." The architect laughed. "One day he will simply explode."

Yaesin turned to the architect. "I don't know who. And what have we to do with other people? We just want a small house, a roof above our head. That is it."

The tall man let go of the branch, sending it swishing back up. Other branches jerked around it, little mulberries fell. The tall man walked back.

"These mulberries are most amazing," he said, still chewing. "It is odd that they should be so good here." He dug some out from his pocket and extended his palm toward the architect and then toward the owner. "Please take some," he said.

The architect picked a few, but Yaesin said no with his head.

"The soil is not right for mulberries," the tall man went on. "And yet, delicious. Strange."

"You have got yourself a nice piece of land," the architect said to Yaesin. And that too from under his tail." He pointed to the neighbor's house.

"Must be biting his nails, that one," the tall man said.

"You will have a beautiful house, YaesinSaeb," the architect said. "Neighbors will burn. Fire engines might have to be called."

Had his wife not stepped in, Yasin might have said something stupid that he would then have regretted immediately. "Didn't you have to meet the person for the shuttering?" she said to her husband. "I hope he hasn't closed already. Five thirty, it was, no?"

"I do," Yaesin said, looking at his watch. "How could I forget!"

He hurried, picking up a few things, a cloth bag, a measuring tape, a small notebook in which he noted the accounts, and hoped that in this sudden hurry to depart he would manage to cause the architect and the tall man to leave too. They couldn't, after all, stay back once the man of the house left.

Manzoor noticed this flurry of movement and looked at the three men walking away. He watched closely as the tall man got on the phone, walking slower than the other two, several steps behind them, and just before he went out through the gate the tall man turned toward Manzoor, waved at him, and said something, too, but Manzoor wasn't sure if he had said it to him or into the phone.

In any case he did not hear anything.

As they walked out the gate, the other laborer was already bending over the hosepipe, washing his hands, his feet, his face. Manzoor urged him to stay back another ten minutes. He had to catch a bus, the other said. "Let's go," he said. "We can have tea on the way."

Manzoor walked up to the owner's wife.

"Don't worry about it," she said. "We will bury it, respectfully, when my husband comes. You go, rest for today. You, too, must be tired."

He looked at her and past her at the tree. "I can dig alone," Manzoor said. "It won't take long."

"In my husband's absence?" She stared at him. "Is that possible? I am a woman, after all. I can't decide on my own. As if you don't know. Can't do anything on my own."

DUSK WAS GATHERING between the tall brick walls. The day was coming to an end, finally. Her husband would return anytime now and they would wrap this thing in a polyethylene bag and then in another bag, and get rid of it. The easiest thing would be to throw it from the bridge. They would have to think about tomorrow, though. What to do with Manzoor? What about the other one? Best would be to get rid of all three, but the head mason, he lived in the same neighborhood, he shouldn't turn vengeful, they would need to ensure that. Maybe she or her husband could fall sick tomorrow. And the work stop for a day. That would give them time. But why hadn't ObduRahim returned from the mosque?

An insect rang somewhere in the distance, an insistent bell, and the birds flying back to their nests cawed together in the sky. Two loads of boulders were coming at ten, and three loads of green rocks after that. So long before the house would be done, before it would actually stand there with the curtains hanging and they could walk in and cook in it and eat in it, and live life without having to worry about so many things, without having to worry about the others. She placed in the basket the blue tea flask, which was still full, and heavy. So much tea wasted. Maybe it could be put to use somehow. The four china cups were untouched, and so the three quarter plates, two spoons, five breads, and the small towel. A cup was missing. She looked around and saw it on the brick near the tree where ObduRahim had been sitting earlier.

The trenches looked deeper at this hour. Two feet would have been enough, perhaps. They wouldn't have encountered anything. But you make a house once, and other things you can change, but the foundation, that can't be changed, the foundation must be strong. The cup was filled almost to the brim. She threw away the tea against the tree, the bark darkening where the tea ran down. Something strange moved on the bark. Two black worms, squirming, twisting their thick soft bodies. She looked at the worms, black, fuzzy, their boneless bodies moving. A shudder climbed up through her. She stepped back, and putting the cup into the basket she walked, quicker than she had all day. Another shudder, violent just like the first. This is what happens, she muttered, this is what happens when you don't spray the trees on time.

Dogs

TWO DOGS WERE WALKING ALONG THE EDGE OF A ROAD. THE one who went with a slight limp turned to the other and said, It is a nice day. Isn't it?

Bigger than the first, and furry, the second dog walked on, quietly, looking at the road ahead of its feet, as if it had heard nothing, but after a moment it raised its head and looked up into the sky. Large bright clouds the color of snow, and a yellow kite midair, its little blue tail fluttering. Birds glided in the distance.

As if it is a spring day, no? the first dog said.

The second nodded. It is, it said, its gaze lingering briefly in the soft blue sky before returning to the road. Is there anything you would like to do, it asked?

They walked slowly, at times beside each other, at times one behind the other, but never too far apart, making way along the narrow edge taken up mostly by people's legs.

Roam around, the first dog said. That would be nice. And maybe, in some time, have a bite too. We could go to the butcher near the dumpster, I like that man, I think he only pretends to hate us. Or maybe, if you prefer, we could even go to that other place, behind the graveyard. Your favorite, remember? It let out a chuckle. Ufff . . . your eyes! How they popped out! I thought your game was over. That bone, what was that? And how could you even put the whole thing in your mouth? I mean, what were you thinking?

The second dog smiled a faint smile.

No, seriously, the first said, what were you thinking?

After a while on the road, the second dog, without looking up, said to the first, Can I tell you something?

Yes, the first replied.

The second dog tried to speak, but no words came. The first turned to look at it. The second tried again. Only the hoarse voices of the vehicles around them.

What? the first asked.

Nothing. The second dog shook its head. Which way should we take?

No, tell, the first insisted. Now my mind won't stop thinking. It will think a thousand things.

They were almost at the busy crossing from which they could go three different ways. Here in the evenings people would stand around burning coals, their faces glowing red, and occasionally they would toss toward the dogs bits of juicy tender meat, and fish too, but the fish sometimes had thorns, sending the dogs barking and spinning like crazy. Those shops still closed at this hour, not one soft morsel lay around; nor was there the enchanting scent of burning flesh that drifted far down the street, and carried even farther into the by-lanes with a little breeze. The dogs could smell only the burnt fumes of gasoline and the rotting stench that rose from the drains open by the side of the road. They halted at the crossing, stood under a billboard on which a large brown cat moved about softly, and a ball rolled in from the corner. If they walked on straight ahead, they would soon be near the parking lot, behind which were the two large dumpsters, and not far from the dumpsters the old graveyard the first dog had mentioned; and if they took the left, they would be walking toward the new shiny building, where before the glass and the lights, the people, the noise, they had spent endless days and nights in the cold, where even many children had been born, and died, but now the doormen would shoo them away from a distance and if somehow they managed to get closer to those tall glass doors that strangely parted open by themselves, the moment their faces appeared in the glass, the doormen would lunge toward them and take such swipes with their long sticks that if, God forbid, one of them fell on their skull, they would from that moment on be walking around with two heads, but what scents of flesh and bone, onions simmering in oil, garlic, shallots, marrow, and so many other unknown smells wafted all day long out of that tall building. The first dog stood uncertain under the changing warm lights of the billboard, divided between taking this road that it liked and taking the road to the right, which curled alongside the park for a while and then passed beside the old bus stand and, after a left and two rights through broken patches, arrived at the chicken seller's and the butcher's small shop where hanging from iron hooks could be legs, ribs, pieces of the back, and in the blue garbage bin by the drain, wings, feet, intestines, and little chicken heads with their eyes open. The air would be thin with a whiff of salt. The second dog knew they would take this road but it waited for the first to make up its mind, and then it followed. They watched carefully for the buses and cars and motorcycles and auto-rickshaws that, shouting and shouting, hurtled madly up and down the wide street.

Tell, the first dog said as they reached the other side.

What? the second replied, its voice barely audible in the noise of the street.

You know what. Tell now. I tell you everything.

I forgot what it was, the second dog said. Perhaps it was nothing.

Come on. You think I am stupid? You shouldn't keep things inside. They cram up. Remember when I hid from you about the fight with the fat dog? It choked me, and the moment I told you and others, it disappeared. Tell. Please.

The second dog walked quietly, looking ahead far into the road, but the first could see hesitation in its face.

Blurt it out, the first said. Just close your eyes and tell.

There is this taste, the second dog said, in my mouth.

What taste? the first asked.

I don't know. Strange taste that won't go away . . . till the back of my tongue, even down my throat sometimes.

Down your throat too? That's odd. What taste is it? Bad taste?

Not down the throat, but just where the throat begins, but I am not sure . . . sometimes it almost goes away, and just when I feel it's gone, it comes again, like . . . like somehow playing a game with me.

I hope it is not like the smell of rotten eggs, I can't stand that from another street.

Not that. The second shook its head. It is not smell.

Oh yes, taste, the first said. What kind of taste is it?

I don't know.

But it must be like something. Like meat? Like chicken? Biscuit? Mud? Salt? Trotters? Blood? Milk? Something? Uttering the name of trotters made the first dog see little sheep trotters in its eyes, and a slow juice oozed into its mouth.

Not like that, the second dog said, not like things we eat. It's like, like something . . . else . . . something that . . . I don't know . . . I don't know like what.

The first dog looked toward the second, but the second did not look back. Maybe it is all the bad food we eat, the first dog said, a trickle of trotter juice still running in its mouth. Everyone says the food has gone bad. No? It could be that, all the bad food going down, leaving a bit of bad taste in our mouth, and then one day making itself felt.

The second dog nodded. Could be, it said. But it knew it was not the food. Or maybe it was. What did it know anyway?

The first dog brought its face closer to the muzzle of the second and sniffed. I can't smell anything on you, though, it said. Your tongue looks fine too. Maybe the color is a little pale, and the pores, they look bigger. Or is this how big pores are? I haven't really looked at them before, it seems, or even the color of tongues. Barely even know the color of my own. It smiled. Are mine so big too?

The second dog looked at the tongue hanging out of the first dog's mouth. A healthy tongue, salivating, orange. Your tongue is fine, it said. I think mine is fine as well, this might just go away by itself. Let's not speak about it anymore.

But at least you still eat, the first dog said. It would be terrible if this taste took away your appetite. You still go at the shank like it is the world between your teeth. That bone, I will never forget that bone in your mouth for the life of me.

But you know . . . The second dog turned to the first. This taste, it somehow . . . somehow . . . everything I . . . it doesn't . . . but to hell with it, maybe I have to learn to live with it, and besides, you are still young, I shouldn't spit at your happiness.

Why do you say that? the first dog protested. I am not as young as you make me out to be. I have been around for a while. Sure, I haven't seen things you have, but I have seen a bit, and I have heard things I haven't seen. We are lucky to be alive. Aren't we?

Motes of dust floated about and as they walked closer to the broken patches, the dust thickened the air. and

"Aren't we," the first dog asked?

I don't know, the second dog said. Honestly I don't remember much anymore. Just fragments, here and there, that don't make much sense.

You can't seriously forget? the first replied. So much happened. So much. I mean even I can't forget! I would never forget. Never! Its narrow face strained with passion, young eyes moistening around the corners, it looked at the second dog. Who would I even be if I forget?

The second dog looked at the first. It nodded but said nothing even though the first expected it to say something. Tears welled up in the eyes of the first. So much happened, the second dog thought, so much, and so much seen, so much spoken, so much heard, so much thought, but as if everything had leaked through, as if inside the head were a hole, leaking things away, quietly, down this dark hole, down and down, leaving behind only bits and pieces that for some reason couldn't go down. A hole in the head, it occurred to the second dog. Could this hole be connected to the hole of the throat and somehow connected to the taste in its mouth? But there was no such hole, or wouldn't it have heard about it from someone, but it need not be a big hole, a very little one, smaller than a tooth even, much smaller, the tip of a thorn. Something itched at the back of its tongue, like a grain of sand. With the saliva in its mouth it tried to swallow the grain, but the grain remained far back on the tongue, just where the tongue seemed to begin. The dog coughed. A hollow sound rising from its throat. It coughed again. Scratching at the back of its tongue with its upper teeth, it gathered a mouthful of spit from all the way back and spat it out; a long transparent thread hung from its lips down to the dust. Bigger than it had earlier been, and rougher, the grain remained there. A fit of coughing took over, hollow sounds convulsing the dog, one cough following another without a pause, interspersed with a barking that sounded no different from the coughing, the dog unable to suppress it even as it tried closing down its mouth.

Are you okay? the first dog asked. Are you okay?

Not knowing what to do, the first dog hovered close, turning its head to look for water. There was no water, just the broken tarmac and the dust swirling out of the huge yellow machines in the distance, their large muddy jaws open. The second dog went on coughing, coughing, and barking at the same time, afraid at one point that its throat might come off with the cough.

The coughing finally stopped, leaving the dog dizzy, its legs weak, a hammer pounding away in its head. Almost the size of a bug, the grain in its dry, bruised throat urged the dog to try again and cough it away. All would be fine if it could only remove this little thing from the back of its tongue. Teeth bound against one another, jaws clenched, eyes filled with water, the second dog held itself from coughing. They started to walk again. The street swam in its eyes. Little puffs of dust rose from under their feet at each step as the dull taste crept up to the upper palate as well.

Every few steps, the first dog glanced toward the second.

I am okay, the second dog said after a while. It was the dust.

But it was bad, it said, I was scared, I thought . . . Its small, dark eyes suddenly lit up. How could I not think of it before? it blurted. What a fool I am! We must go and see the old dog. How did I not think of it earlier!

No, the second dog said. Let's not do that.

Why not? I, too, want to show my leg. It aches all the time. Gives me such discomfort. And we aren't far from there. Through the park and we will be there in no time. There wouldn't be this dust either. Besides, the old dog knows you. That is better than if I just show up by myself.

I am already feeling better, the second dog tried to convince the first. Let's just roam around, as you said.

But we are roaming around. What else are we doing? Let's say we roam around toward its tree, and if it is there, we say hello, and if not, we just keep roaming on till the butcher's. Please, let's go. This leg gives me so much trouble, the first dog said, walking now with an exaggerated limp. Please.

The second dog had not spoken to the old dog in a long time. If they ever crossed paths deep in some alleyway or on some busy street, the second dog pretended not to have seen the old dog. The old dog did the same. To now sit beneath the old dog's tree and tell it about the taste in its mouth, to open its jaws wide, stick out its tongue, to lay itself out there, the thought made it feel sicker. But when the first dog squeezed through the rusty turnstile of the park, the second quietly followed, twisting its body to get through the iron bars that smelled of grease and people's palms.

Two enormous trees rose high, their wide branches and pale leaves hiding the sky, hiding the clouds. The dogs walked in the shadow of the trees, over brittle leaves scattered on the ground, past an old couple who sat on the grass beside a bed of geraniums. A half-eaten biscuit between her fingers, the woman stared absently into the distance, and then said something to the man, making him laugh. The woman laughed as well, slapped at the man's knee with her hand. She put the biscuit in her mouth. The first dog felt its mouth salivating, but they kept on walking along the narrow brick path that curled toward the fountain around a tall green bush. They could already hear the water as they passed the tall magnolia tree, passed the barberry hedges. They climbed up the three stone steps to the pool, where, from the broken nozzle, water gurgled into the bowl of the fountain. Crouching over the water, they cleared away with their muzzles the leaves floating on the surface. The water was dark and cool. The second dog saw its own reflection in the water, tongue hanging out of its mouth, eyes vaguely visible. it seemed he had lost weight. Or was he losing hair? Suddenly the water jerked away, and tore, and a thousand drops hit it in the face and on the neck and on its body. Its head dipped into the water, the first dog was flapping its ears, creating a pool full of bubbles, a bubble pool. When it brought its head out, the hair was all wet, its nose dripping, its mouth pulled into a beautiful foolish smile.

The water is so cool, it said.

The second dog smiled back at it, and gently dipped its mouth into the water and lapped up a mouthful. The water wet its parched throat, and it immediately drank another mouthful, this time holding the water for a while in its mouth, moistening each pore on its tongue, allowing it to seep through the surface down to the roots, to cleanse its mouth of everything. The grain dissolved away, leaving behind just the tongue. Relieved, it drank another gulp, held it in its mouth, and muzzle facing the sky, eyes closed, it gurgled, and gurgled again, and then swallowed the water. The tongue cool and wet, the palate wet, the throat wet, but the dull taste stubbornly remaining behind near the back of its tongue, as if the water could merely pass over it. No longer thirsty, the dog looked into the water, waiting for the ripples to die away, wanting to see its tongue.

Let's go in, the first dog yelled, its hair still dripping drops of water. Let's jump.

The second dog looked into its shining eyes. You go, it said. I will be here.

Come on, the first replied. This is nice. This is so nice. It will make you feel better.

The second shook its head. You go. I will join in a while. Go.

The second dog wanted to lie somewhere in the shade, hide its mouth near its chest, close its eyes. If it closed its eyes long enough, and arrived in its mind at a silence away from all this noise, it might be able to find the exact point from where the taste rose, and then it might be able to do something about it. Maybe it really was a passing thing, maybe it was all in its head, but this strange feeling in the heart, this sense of something, maybe this too was a passing thing. And why not?

Someone barked. Wowww, woww.

The dogs looked around furtively. From behind tall yellow sunflowers a few young boys were looking at them. Bags slung across their backs, faces illuminated, eyes twinkling, they barked again. One of the boys dropped his bag onto the grass and in a quick familiar movement picked up something and then pulled back his arm behind his head.

Stones hit the electric pole, the broken fountain, the trunk of the magnolia tree. One whizzed past the ear of the first dog; another hit the tail of the second. The stones flew toward them at great speed but they were pebbles really, except from one of the boys who threw nothing less than the size of an egg. Barking, yelling, cursing, the dogs ran in circles, around the trees, around the fountain, around the bush, their vision blurred, their legs slipping under them. The boys spread out and surrounded the dogs, the old couple got to their feet, the man picked a stone, the woman clutched tighter at the packet of biscuits, she picked up something too, but they did not throw. Two of the boys, though, went on throwing, and the dogs ran farther and farther till with a frantic leap the second dog hurled itself over the run-down trellis into the overgrown bush. Right behind the second dog, on top of its back, fell the first. Their convulsing bodies met on all sides with sharp piercing things, and they jerked and tossed about and howled for a while, but once they became still and their eyes adjusted to the dimness inside the bush, they saw a thin pathway. The second dog could barely breathe, but saving themselves from the tangles, the thorns, the thistles, and the occasional stone that still landed through the leaves, they walked through the narrow tunnel carved into the bush by the bodies of other dogs.

Where are we going? the first dog whispered.

We will see, the second said. Its tongue hanging out, and still out of breath, it walked ahead of the first. Are you hurt? it asked.

No, the first said. And you? You hurt?

The second shook its head.

They arrived at a little clearing inside the bush, a small round patch surrounded by dark green leaves, and canopied by the leaves; they stopped, turned to face each other, listened.

Are you okay? the first dog asked.

Yes, the second dog replied.

There were no more voices. No stones sounded through the foliage. A heavy scent lurked in the cramped silence, of honey and cinnamon, and of leaves that had fallen and decayed on the sunless earth; from beneath the leaves rose a faint smell of urine that made the first dog aware of the urine urging inside it. The dog let it pass, its eyes vacant with relief, the sound of the urine the only sound, froth rising on the earth beneath the dog's feet and, above it, thin wisps of vapor.

The first dog smiled. Don't you want to pee?

No, the second said. The second dog led the way through the little tunnel that curled right and narrowed to a small hole, clumps of leaves brushing against their faces, branches, twigs poking into necks and ribs, their feet stepping into dead vines. The second dog bit on a broad green leaf, tore it away, chewed it between its teeth. Bitterness spread like a stain on its tongue. It had been foolish to cut through the park at this hour, too many people with nothing to do and, in their boredom, doing anything. Thank God people's aim was not good enough; if only they could hit what they wanted, how terrible would it be. But how had they both escaped without being hit despite so many stones? Had they really dodged them all? But they had been barely aware, just running and running. Or could it be that the boys were not really aiming at them? They had been, though, they had. So strange that they hadn't been hit, and survived whole except for this exhaustion from all the running that had gone into saving themselves.

One after the other, twisting their bodies, the two dogs made their way through the bright little hole in the brick wall that put a quick end to the bush.

Do you know where we are going? the first dog asked as it emerged on the other side.

I think so, the second said, looking at the empty lot, overgrown with trees and weeds and tall grass and littered with garbage and broken-down vehicles around which plants had grown to the windows.

Where *are* we? the first asked. I have never been here. And which way is the old dog's tree?

On the other side, the second dog said. This is the backside. You will need to go behind that bus and then carry on farther.

I will need to? The first dog turned to the second. Don't say I will need to, I swear I won't go alone. You have to come with me, that was our deal.

I am tired, the second dog said. I will rest.

Then I will rest with you, the first replied, but I am not going without you.

This side of the park was lower by a few feet, and the dogs had to leap down to the ground. They walked slowly amid the tall grasses, skirting around a mound of debris that stank of rotten waste and shit.

There! the first dog shouted. Look!

Behind a rusted olive-green vehicle, they saw the head of a brown dog they knew from the bone place near the dumpster, where it came often with its three puppies.

What is it doing here? the first said. It was hopping now, the limp turning into a skip in its step. Come, come, it said to the second, you are not tired, are you? Just a little more and we are there.

The second dragged behind it. In the distance, barely visible in the grass, the second dog glimpsed another head. A thirst rose in its throat, its bitter mouth stank, its stomach churned. It spat out the remains of the leaf. There was nothing except the saliva tinged green. It did not want to walk any farther, did not want to walk to the old dog, did not want to go to the butcher even; on what legs it carried on, it itself didn't know. It wanted to lie down, bury its face in the grass, and in the damp coolness of the earth close to the roots of the grass forget about everything, and yet it wanted someone to be nearby.

EYES CLOSED, body curled into a misshapen ball, the old dog lay beneath the willow tree in a shallow concavity in the ground. The two dogs walked toward it, and as they walked, they became aware of other dogs all around, far to the left and the right, their still bodies half hidden in the tall grass. Some of them emaciated, some that were healthy, and one, beside an abandoned jeep, so fat that it seemed to be standing on a chicken's legs. The first dog immediately recognized it, they had fought near the dumpster in bitter cold, then by the banks of the river. What was it doing here? Even fatter than it had been then, the first dog thought, it would be a miracle if it could walk two steps. The fat dog, though, paid no attention to anything, not even seeing the two dogs as they passed the line of his gaze

The first dog murmured a greeting. The old dog did not open its eyes, did not respond, remaining motionless except for the rising and falling of its chest and the breath escaping its mouth with a muffled whistle. The first dog turned to the brown dog and smiled at it, the brown dog did not smile back. It murmured the greeting again. No one replied. It was quiet here, the sounds of the street a distant hum, the quiet at once peaceful and ominous. The first dog turned to the second, the second gestured for it to sit.

Did you lose your way? the old dog creaked. Its eyes opened briefly through lashes so white that the first dog had never seen anything like it. Its eyes, old and pale, looked from behind a fog, and then closed again.

We were passing by, the first dog replied, and we thought of visiting you. My uncle often mentions you, says you and my great-grandfather knew each other well.

The second dog remained quiet, looking at the loose charcoal skin on the old dog's back, thin and hairless like a worn-out rag. On its neck remained a tuft of forgotten hair that looked worse than the bare dying skin. In the dust between its legs a gray old scrotum lay like a burnt stone.

Smiling uncertainly, the first dog said its uncle would be glad to know it had visited the old dog. The old dog did not respond, and in the silence the first dog looked toward the second, urging it with its eyes to speak. The second dog looked down.

Also, it's my leg, the first dog said. I wanted to show it to you. It aches. The first dog put out its left foreleg, touched with its muzzle near the left knee. Here. It comes suddenly, the first dog said, the pain. Sometimes wakes me in the night. Now it is not as bad, though. It was worse when I was hit. Now it just sometimes stabs at me. Especially in the night.

Soak it in small puddles when the sun is high, the old dog said without opening its eyes. Keep warm when it is too cold. And don't run too fast. Don't fly. And stretch your body like someone is pulling your forelegs from the front and your hind legs from behind. Come to see me on the next half-moon. Also, it is a good thing to bring something along. It was fine to just show up without anything in the old days, but now it is bad manners.

The first dog lowered its head. I will bring something the next time. We came today without a plan.

It is not for me, the old dog said. It is for others. Do you understand? I don't keep anything for myself, despite what some dogs might tell you. And even if I keep a thing or two, what's wrong in that? It gets so cold in the winter, and I am no puppy anymore, why not have a couple of those nice soft blankets? How long must we sleep in the open with nothing under us, nothing above us? I would suggest you get yourself a bit of a blanket too. It would do your leg a lot of good. Do you understand?

I do, the first dog said.

The grass rustling about it, the brown dog walked toward them but stopped a few paces away. The old dog did not look at it, as if it had forgotten about it. It was the second dog, whose mouth after the bitterness of the leaf had returned to its own dull taste, who looked at it. The brown dog looked weak and tired. It looked back at the second dog.

Sit, the second dog said to it.

The old dog's tail moved in the dust. Sit, it said. Sit if you like.

The brown dog remained standing.

It does not want to sit, the old dog said to the second dog. Let it be. It is grieving.

What for? the second dog asked.

What does one grieve for? The old dog opened its eyes and looked at the second dog. For oneself, the old dog said. No?

The second dog said nothing, but the ease with which it had been seen through stabbed into it. Its tongue lay heavy in its mouth like a dead thing.

Its kid died a few days ago, the old dog said. Under a truck. It sat by the little thing for two whole days, but eventually one needs to get up. But where does one go from there? So it came here. And here it is.

The second dog remembered the three fawn puppies and wondered which of them was dead. Not that it mattered. Someone died all the time. That was that. Unless it looked at the brown dog, looked into its eyes, and opened itself, allowed itself to see on the street a small dead puppy in a little pool of its own blood, allowed that image to press against its own eyes, and saw the dog beside the pup, and then the torn pup by itself, vanishing away slowly to a stain and then turning, in the sun and rain and under the cars that went without knowing anything, to nothing. Only then did the pup become real, only then did the brown dog become real, but why look into its eyes, useless, to bring a dead thing to life. The dead are for the dead.

It has not sat down since it came here, the old dog said, not eaten a blade of grass, not spoken a single word. And there will come a moment, I don't know when or maybe I do, when its legs will no longer hold its weight and it will shatter to the ground, and for a long time it will weep and then it will sleep. When it wakes up, it will have forgotten everything.

And I don't care what stories anyone goes around telling, the old dog said, that I hate dogs, that I punish them, that I kill them.

Are you sure it can get back on its legs again? the second dog asked despite itself.

You are a butcher, the old dog said, you and your ilk. Knife in hand, striking at everything that does not fit to your narrow eyes. What do you know about healing? Why don't you try healing it? When your fate turns upside down, it becomes your fate to be toyed with by everyone. How do you think you would console it? By telling the truth, and what might that be? A good lie is, any day, better than the truth. Even more so because who knows the truth? Walking around with pups half your age, putting your wretched weight on them, eating away at whatever happiness might come their way, I hope you don't think that is the truth. Its kid dies, it comes here, what for? So I can ease its heart? Lighten the burden of a dead puppy? Do I have some magic here? Does God sit by my side and leave me magic bones? Besides, I need my own consolation. But you wouldn't get it. You are just a bitter old dog peeing on other people's bones. Let's move on with it, the old dog said. I don't think you came here for nothing. Seems to me you are dying. Are you? Your face is pale and light has left your eyes. Your hair is shedding too. You don't have much longer. Is that it?

The second dog looked at the old dog in a light that seemed to have dimmed.

You don't want to move, do you?

Maybe, the second dog said. But that way, shouldn't you have died a long time ago?

The old dog laughed. You still haven't learned anything, have you? You simply say what comes into your mind. Like a pup born last week. Maybe I am dying, or even dead, do you think everyone dies the same way? You don't still think it is those wretched hiccups and the closing of eyes, do you, the lying there like a stone? If only dying were so easy.

The Man with the Suitcase

THE FIRST TIME HE SAW THE MAN, SALIM WAS HIDING UNDER the awning of a shoe shop. It was raining one of those rains that last five minutes but drench everything, making everyone run for shelter. The woman beside Salim looked up the entire time, asking God for pity. Loose ends of wet hair stuck to her face. "First he pours it in silence for two days," she said, turning to Salim. "Now he tears the sky open. Our own sins." Across the street Salim saw the man, pressed in with a dozen people under the canopy of the bakery shop, shaking rain off his long black umbrella.

Even with the distance of the wide road and the rain lashing down, Salim saw him more clearly than he had seen anyone in a while. Somehow he stood out with his gray hair, checkered shirt, dark pants. It was, probably, the suitcase in his hand. A brown leather suitcase that others might have paid no attention to, but Salim, having worked for a year at the luggage store, saw it immediately. The man was looking around, at the sky, at the street, at the people on the other side, and for one moment Salim felt the man's eyes rest on him, and then they moved on. Salim went on looking at him, though, woken as if from a long sleep full of dreams, or was it yet another dream he was slipping into, waking briefly as he passed through the doorway between two dreams?

Someone tugged at Salim's jacket; it was the woman. "Four days ago," she said, "even before the first drop, I dreamt of boats rowing here, everywhere. Even electric wires weren't visible. Just water." Drops of rain emerged from her gray hair and crawled down her forehead, down the sharp ridge of her nose. She said something more, about birds, about dogs, about children, and Salim looked at her creased face, at the opening and closing of her thin lips, but he no longer heard her. By the time he looked back across the street the man was gone, a narrow emptiness where he had been. He was nowhere on the road, where people were returning under their umbrellas. Salim searched among the walking legs but no sign of the brown suitcase. The woman shook open her umbrella and stepped off the footpath. The street began to fill again, the warm awnings emptied out. His hands buried in the pockets of the oversized blue jacket that had belonged to his brother, Salim walked into the drizzle.

FOR SEVERAL DAYS NOW—EIGHT or ten or twelve, he was no longer sure—Salim had been showing up at random shops, asking if they required a salesman. He left home in the mornings and returned in the evenings, spending his days on the streets. His family thought that he still worked at the luggage store in the busy market in the center of the city where he had worked for almost a year, taking up the place that had earlier been his brother Farooq's, till the owner of the store, one late afternoon, took him aside. They weren't doing good business, the owner said, so having two salesmen made no sense. Salim wasn't surprised. Twice over that month the owner had asked him about his sales for the day, and there hadn't been much, a faux leather pouch one time, a small canvas bag the second. The other salesman, who had worked at the store for more than fifteen years, always had things to show. "You don't watch the customer carefully," the owner told Salim, "so you never grab him at the right moment, and if you are not interested in the customer, I am not interested in you."

The only person he had visited before leaving that market was Nazir at the radio store just across the narrow street. Nazir was sitting behind the wooden counter, counting money. An old song played from one of the radio sets.

"Did you close already?" Nazir asked, looking up for a moment.

"No."

"Did Butterhead ask you to leave?"

Salim did not answer. He sat quiet on the round stool.

Nazir looked at him while his index finger rose and fell through a handful of 500 rupee notes like that of a man who had counted a lot of money in his life. When he finished, he lit a cigarette and leaned back in his chair. "Now?" he asked.

Salim remained silent, looking down.

"What are you hanging your head for, like some bride? Raise your head."

Nazir was older, around seventy, but he didn't seem like an old man. He was always joking in his loud voice, calling people names, and smoking more cigarettes than anyone in the market, swearing on his knee that he would quit soon. When Farooq had died, Nazir had visited their home twice, both times asking Salim to call on him if he needed anything. Salim knew he meant it. And when Salim came to work here at the market, he had found Nazir warm and funny.

"You are sleeping," Nazir had said, "and it won't do. You are not a child, Salim. You have a family, old parents, younger sister. And your own self! How old are you, anyway? Twenty-six? Twenty-seven?" Nazir extinguished the cigarette, almost violently, against the blackened wood of an ashtray and then dropped it among the bent stubs. "We must accept his will and move on," he said. "What else can we do?"

Nazir was a gambler. He came to the market some days on a run-down scooter and sometimes in a big car. The luggage store owner had once said that Nazir turned into a different man when he was gambling. "Like a man possessed. Those small eyes become big, and he can bet anything then, car, scooter, anything, even if you are sitting beside him."

His thick hairy arms resting on the counter, Nazir lit another cigarette. He had this wild look in his small glassy eyes, and with those eyes and the cigarette and the short white beard he looked old and young at the same time. "Go to another market. You can be a good salesman, but only if you wake up. This is not your home, Salim, this is not your neighborhood. Remember that. This is the market, this is the world, and it doesn't care."

As Salim rose to leave, Nazir passed him five hundred-rupee notes. Salim refused, but Nazir insisted. "You will need it," he said, holding out the crisp notes. "You are the man in your house now. Pretend till you become one."

SOME SHOPKEEPERS SAID NO without looking at him, and others looked at his face for a while and then said no. It was strange to be looked at like that, as if something were written on his forehead. Loose change weighing down one pocket, a few crumpled tenners in the other, and the one hundred-note left in his wallet not so crisp anymore, the money Nazir had given was running out. The rain had stopped, leaving behind dark pools in the craters of the wet road. Salim walked along the edge, avoiding the puddles and the barely-moving cars that honked endlessly.

Lights came on in the street and then, one after another, in the shops and on the billboards. Pale, orange, white, the street looked smaller suddenly, warmer, reminding him of his old market, which he had avoided since losing the job. He missed Nazir's stories and his jokes, he missed Khaliq's cigarette kiosk and the little tea shop, he missed sitting in the luggage store surrounded by suitcases and bags and the smell of fake leather that used to oppress him, he even missed the old owner, who was not a bad person, paying salaries on time and always ordering tea for the salesmen when he ordered one for himself. But while he missed it, he did not long to return to it, missing it rather like something that was gone.

He spotted the shop from a distance, a large cone of ice cream glowing on its billboard. It looked full of customers, which was odd with all the rain. He passed it, walked over to the corner kiosk, and counting change on his wet palm, bought a cheap cigarette. He walked on toward the curling alleyway full of bright garment shops, none of which needed a salesman.

The first breath of smoke settled something within him. He looked around, at the people, at the cars, at the lights reflecting in the wet tarmac, at the feet rising and falling. Their handcarts covered with transparent plastic sheets, the cart sellers hawked apples, pears, rubber boots, plastic jackets. People passed by talking of the rain, and of the water rising in the river, and every now and then they looked up toward the sky. Strangled by old clouds, the sky was gray and heavy, like the sodden branches of the trees. The downpour had brought with it evening. He must get home soon, or his mother would worry herself, and everyone else. If she hadn't already! Another hour, this one shop, maybe it would all work out here. He took a long last drag and walked toward the ice cream shop, and just as he was about to enter, he saw the man on the other side of the road coming along with the suitcase, and again he felt that waking sensation. The man walked carefully on the busy footpath, holding a black umbrella over his head. Salim felt a pull toward him. Had he not been at the door of the shop and reminded himself that he needed a job, he might have allowed himself to be led; and though he walked into the ice cream shop, a part of him had left after the man.

THE MAN AT the counter smiled as Salim approached. "What would you like?"

"I am looking for a job," Salim said. "I heard you might have a place."

The man pursed his lips and looked at Salim. "What would you like?" He smiled, his gaze shifting slightly. A young couple stood beside Salim.

"Softy," the boy said, and then looked at the girl, and she too said, "Softy."

"We have vanilla, butterscotch, fig and honey, chocolate chip, and strawberry."

The couple looked at each other again and smiled.

"Tell," the boy said to the girl.

She smiled. "Strawberry."

"One strawberry and one vanilla," the boy said to the man.

"No, no," the girl said. "I will also have vanilla."

"Are you sure?" the boy asked.

"Yes." She smiled. He smiled too.

"Two vanillas, then," the shopkeeper said, pointing toward two empty seats in the crowded shop.

The man looked again at Salim. "What would you like?"

Three young men stood behind him this time, and he shifted a little to make space, moving into the corner. The shop looked even more crowded from the corner. The only opening was the glass door onto the street. The three took time deciding, talking loudly, mango shake, banana shake, Oreo, one of them turning around his finger a key chain with a small red boxing glove at the end. Something tightened within Salim, he felt a lack of air, and under the white bulbs that lit the windowless shop, gloom gathered inside him again. The voices that rose from the tables, the laughter, the sighs, glass mugs rising and resting back, the chewing, the sipping, the slurping, the screeching of the plastic legs of the chairs, they all assembled into a dull noise that rose like a groan from somewhere deep below, and Salim wanted to run out into the rain outside, to fill his chest with air, to breathe.

He found the shopkeeper looking at him, and for some reason he looked down, avoiding the shopkeeper's eyes.

Someone else came in, and then someone else, and the shopkeeper seemed no longer to remember Salim, who was standing beside him in the corner, till on the footpath outside, walking just beside the glass door of the shop, Salim saw the man again. For a moment he thought the man was stepping in for an ice cream, but he walked on, the brown leather suitcase almost rubbing against the door. Salim slowly made his way out of the corner, and just as he reached the door, the shopkeeper called after him.

"If you really needed the job," the shopkeeper said, "you would have stayed for two more hours. Until we closed. Those who need a job, they wait."

He was looking at Salim. Salim looked back, blocking the way for a couple who wanted to get to the counter.

"Go, go," the shopkeeper said. "Show those eyes to someone else."

Salim stood where he was, staring. A listless anger rising inside him that only made him hate the place more.

"Don't stand blocking the way now," the shopkeeper said. "God help you with finding a job. We don't have one for you."

He walked around blindly, humiliated, as much at the insult as at the fact that he had just walked away. What could he have said, though? What was there to say? There was no desire in him to go back and avenge the insult, but he felt shame, deepening with every step. He no longer felt any impulse to look for the man with the suitcase, this man who moments ago had pulled at him, made his feet move from the corner. He felt nothing for him.

WHEN THE RAIN began again, Salim was halfway home, hanging by the iron railings at the back of the crowded bus. He tightened his grip on the slippery metal, planted his feet more firmly, like the other men hanging beside him, their hands and feet inches from one another. The wiry bus conductor went on shouting the names of the places along the route. Every few minutes he drew his lower lip in and whistled, bringing the bus to a halt, and then he jumped off, collecting fares and returning the change, and carving space for yet another passenger, and then, whistling the bus back to life, he hopped onto the railing. "No respite!" he said to Salim. "The flood is due. And why not?" His wet hair rising like bristles, he looked younger than Salim. "If I tell you what I see every day, with my own eyes, on the back seat, boys and girls, no one else, our sisters, you won't believe. Now God has come to settle the account. What else will happen!"

Barely holding on with two fingers, he was at ease on the railing, humming a song, swaying a little. Salim imagined himself taking the conductor's place, but Salim couldn't even whistle properly, nothing that would reach above the noise of the street from the back of the speeding bus to the driver up there at the front. Farooq's whistle would have covered the distance, though, that long piercing sound he made with his thumb and index finger between his lips. Very clearly, he heard Farooq's whistle fly through his head, a sound he had not heard in a long time. It reminded him of days with Farooq in the house, walking into the kitchen, stepping out of the bathroom, roaming about the yard in the sun. He tried to hear the whistle again, waited for it to rise in his head, but instead the conductor whistled, and the bus slowed down.

THE DARK FIGURE of his mother loomed near the gate of their house. He saw her from a distance. When she had started waiting at the gate, Salim thought it would last a week, or maybe a month, but almost ten months had passed since Farooq had been killed. Earlier he had shouted at his mother that it made no sense to wait outside, to ask every passerby if things were fine in the city; the neighbors too had sons working in the city, after all, and if he made it safely to their lane, he would reach home too; and if he, too, had to die, her standing at the gate wouldn't save him. One evening, he had pushed her in from the gate, her frail shoulder going along with the force of his hand. The scarf had fallen off her head, and with her thin gray and white braid quivering behind her like the tail of a rat, she scurried in, raising both her hands to cover her face, as if Salim would have slapped her. The next day she was there again.

"Is it you, Salim?" she asked when he reached closer.

"Yes," he said.

"Thank God." She patted him on the shoulder. "I was worried. Come in, come in. You are all wet."

He walked behind her, and pulled at the soggy towel that covered her head and her shoulders.

"I just came out," she said. "Not even a minute ago."

Salim said nothing.

His father sat in the corner in the kitchen. The radio whispered beside him. He could usually be found in that corner or lying in the sun on the front porch, or standing at one of the shop fronts in the small neighborhood market, talking with someone or other.

"Everything remained fine in the city?" the father asked.

"Yes," Salim said.

"Did it rain hard there?"

"Yes."

"Here it cut open the earth. God's wrath, nothing else," the father said. "They are saying on the radio that there will be a huge flood if it keeps raining."

Salim's sister took his jacket and handed him a towel. Only now did he feel how cold and wet he was.

"The rich will climb on their upper floors," the father said. "Where will the poor go? And God will go on thinking he brought the flood for everyone. The rich will trick even God."

"God is of the poor too," Salim's mother said. "He will protect everyone."

"God of the poor is poor himself," the father replied, returning to his radio.

His father had been a carpenter, working mostly on the roofs, till he fell down one day, thankfully onto the first-floor balcony and not on the rocks on the ground. The fall broke his back, and when he recovered after five long months, he could not return to carpentry. Instead, he hung about in the market outside, often sitting on the footpath of the same shop that had once been his, where many years ago, when Salim and Farooq were still young, he had unsuccessfully tried to sell first vegetables and then charcoal. "Selling the shop, the biggest mistake of my life," he repeated every day. "But that money helped build the house," he added in the next breath. "When you go to sell, it fetches nothing, and when you go to buy, it costs everything." "Why don't you find a job?" his wife had once suggested. "Thank God, your back is fine now." He had looked at her as if he had been pushed down from a roof again. "I have broken my back working all my life," he had replied. "Made this house, raised the children. Now I am an old man waiting for death." And that was the end of it. Farooq had still been alive then, working at the luggage store, and he had asked the mother not to bring up the job again. "We will manage," he had said. Salim had just started out then, as a salesman at an electronics shop that closed down not long after it opened.

The four of them were sitting cross-legged around the sheet for dinner. "Take another egg," his mother said to Salim. They sat looser since Farooq's death, and yet a space seemed vacant. "Your sister cooked the eggs for you. You like them. Don't you?"

"Yes, they are good."

He did like them, but it was Farooq who loved the fried boiled eggs cooked with tomatoes. He could eat three of these for dinner. Sometimes he would ask the sister to look at the spider on the ceiling, and then steal from her plate. She had been close to Farooq, asking him for things, money for a dress, for shoes, money to go to the sewing school. She never asked anything from Salim.

"Is it not good?" the sister asked.

"It is." He took another egg.

They treated him now like he was Salim and Farooq both, while he was barely even Salim anymore. They had hoped that the two brothers would haul the family out of the tightness of their circumstances and bring them closer to the position of their relatives, who lived in the same neighborhood, toward a painted two-story house, a tiled pavement, a car, a good match for the sister, and the respect that came along with those things. But here he was, uneducated really, having stopped at the twelfth grade, and jobless, while one of his cousins worked at the bank now, and another who had been a friend in childhood was in Dubai and seemed to have forgotten that they had ever been friends. Salim's father said that this cousin sent so much money from Dubai that the family could no longer see. "Fat has grown on their eyes," he said.

HE HAD HIS ROOM in the upper floor of the house. There was nothing else on that floor; even his room was not much of anything, four bare walls, cemented and cold, and a bulb hanging from a wire in the middle. They used this room to store onions and potatoes and coals in the winter. Garlands of dried tomatoes and turnips still hung from the long iron nails in the walls, and Salim's shirts and pants hung on the nails beside them. In the corner was a tall stack of heavy winter bedding, and in a wicker basket, potatoes. How glad he was to have this small room, though, where he was cold even under two quilts in the winter; how glad to have some space away from the arguments, and the silences, and the conversations about the relatives and the neighbors, the sighs and the mourning, separated from it all at least by the distance of a staircase.

When he closed his eyes that night, he saw the rain-drenched streets from the day, and the stores, the people, the wet face of the woman, the man walking the street with the suitcase. The ice cream shop owner showed up as well, his face a mere flash but enough to make Salim feel something lodged in his chest. He turned to the other side, his face against the pillow, and tried to remember the man, and the suitcase, the brown leather, the straps.

The rain fell on the tin roof with a gentle patter, like pigeons pecking at grain. He turned again, hoping to arrive at sleep. In the morning he would find it hard to wake up, to tear away from the warmth of the same quilts in which each night he struggled to find sleep. He lit a cigarette, got up from the mattress on the floor, and walked over to the window. Rain. Slow, soft rain falling in the pale glow of the moon that hung in the sky like a large lamp. Everything was washed, everything clean, the trees with their dark sinewy bark, their leaves, the brick walls fixed with glass shards on top, the sad face of the neighbor's house hunched in the rain, wrapped about itself, curtains drawn on its big windows, water falling from the gutters on the roof. Drops of water crawled down the glass panes, and it calmed him to press his face against the window and watch the rain fall.

THE LIGHT BLUE SUITCASE lay open in the kitchen, spread in the middle of the sitting area, eating up half the space. It was strange to see it there, as if it had been kept there on purpose.

"Why is this here?" he asked his mother.

"I don't know," she replied, not looking up from the spinach she was cleaning. "Your father was looking for something."

He could tell that they had had an argument, and was glad that it had already happened, and that his father was not there now.

"Left this mess here in the morning," she said, "and now has gone to dig into who knows what. When people have no work, this is what they do."

Salim sat against the wall, stretched his legs. He was surprised at how deep the suitcase was and how it almost doubled with the two halves parted. He poured himself tea and looked through the scatter of prescriptions and receipts and old photos that his father had left beside the suitcase. Beneath a large tree Farooq was smiling. He wondered where the picture had been taken. Nishat, perhaps, or Shalimar. In the next photo, Farooq, in the same blue jeans and untucked cream shirt, sat with his feet dipped in a wide stream. Salim had seen these photos after Farooq's death, when they were looking for pictures to give to the journalists. He wondered if there was a picture of them together. He couldn't remember them taking one. Farooq had been four years older than him, but Salim had never recognized the seniority of those years, had been reluctant to give the respect, the obedience everyone seemed to expect from him for the elder brother. He had fought with Farooq since they were young, and at some point they stopped speaking to each other, and when they did rarely speak, addressing each other in a slanted, misdirected way, their words were strung together by a tense awkwardness. They often talked through their sister or mother. Even when they had brought his body home, Salim and Farooq hadn't spoken in a long time. He had felt an urge to speak then, with Farooq lying dark and bloodied on the wooden plank, but there was nothing to say. Like everyone, he could only weep. Now, among the photos and documents left beside the suitcase, he found a photo with all of them, in their backyard, the sun shining on their faces. It surprised him how young Farooq looked in the picture. He had never seen him young like this. Beneath the transparent plastic bag that held the papers for the land and their house, wrapped in a white bag were the folded newspapers. Despite himself, he opened the bag. On one of the papers was a picture of his mother and sister crying, and his brother's face lay small in a box beside them. "Man Killed by Government Forces," the headline read. In the other paper, he saw his own picture, sitting beside the father on their porch.

"Everyone is stocking up, one can't trust the rain," his mother said. "Ask the owner to pay you early this time. We should have some money at home."

"I will," he replied. He put the papers back in the bag, and, not wanting his mother to see them, found an envelope in which he put Farooq's photos.

WATER FLOWED LIKE shallow brooks through the streets of the city. On the footpath people walked under umbrellas. Salim, again without one, covered his head with the hood of the jacket. He thought of visiting Nazir at the radio store, to borrow some more money. He knew Nazir wouldn't refuse him the money, and besides he wouldn't ask for too much. Should he go to see Nazir, or visit a few shops first? But who would hire a salesman in this rain?

The owner of the stationery shop said no as if Salim were a beggar, making a gesture for him to leave with the back of his hand. They were moving cartons of paper to the upper shelves. Then the older man standing there called him back. "We don't want a salesman," he said, "but we can hire you to carry these boxes to the godown. There is the cart." He pointed at a handcart covered with a yellow tarpaulin. Salim saw himself pushing it through the city's streets. "The godown is not that far, and you have to carry them up to the third floor. There will be two of those carts at most. I will give you 300."

Salim thought about it for a moment. The old man watched him. "I will do it," Salim said.

"Don't get the cartons wet, though," the old man said. "It is paper. If water seeps in, the whole thing is lost." The other man, who had said no to Salim, called to a third man, who was up on the ladder, and asked him to accompany Salim.

One of the wheels kept veering toward the left, making the cart heavier than it ought to be. "It is going to flood," the man accompanying Salim said. "It seems so," Salim answered, his head covered by a yellow gunnysack that the shop owner had handed him. The other man was a salesman at the stationery shop. They had two more salesmen, the man said. But they were helping at the second shop in another market that was lower and had more chances of flooding.

Salim saw himself pushing that cart through the city, the torn gunnysack covering his head. The gunnysack reminded him of an older relative who had been a laborer, carrying bricks and rocks and sand. He had worked at their house too, and Salim remembered that his hands had looked like feet and his feet shapeless like clods of mud, as if his bare feet had pulled up mud with them at every step and that mud never fell off. Even at weddings, the man had looked like a laborer, and everyone said he worked like a donkey. The godown was far and the steps of the building steep. They carried one carton after the other to the large room already half filled with stacks of similar cartons. The room had large windows, and a few of the panes were broken and covered with plastic sheets. After they were done with the cartons, Salim walked over to the window, brought out a cigarette. The salesman asked if he had another. Salim didn't. Standing by the window, they shared the cigarette. Salim was looking out and listening to the man talk about a flood many years ago that drowned the stationery shop when, down in the alley, he glimpsed the suitcase again. He thought at first that it was someone else under the umbrella with a flat wool cap, but he recognized the suitcase. He told the salesman he had lost his wallet and he ran, saying he would be back. He ran down the stairs, past the cart, and into the street, in the same direction he had seen the man go. When he got out of the lane, onto the main street, he looked right and left, and took the left, believing the man to have gone that way. Far away, Salim saw the man, ascending the bridge. Salim hurried, unaware of the sack on his head, till at some point he felt it rub against his neck and pulled it off. This time he was not going to lose him. The man walked up the bridge that arched over the river and led into the heart of the city. Salim ran. The walkway was full of people looking down at the river. The man, too, halted at an empty spot by the railing and looked down. Salim stood a few paces away; he, too, turned to look through the wire mesh at the swollen dark brown river, flowing just beneath the bridge, hurtling along big branches and rags, and trash and trash.

"They fixed this mesh here," one of the men in the crowd said, shaking the wire mesh with his hand, "to stop people from jumping in the river, and here comes the river now. Do they have a wire mesh for that?"

Salim kept his eyes on the man this time. He wore the same shirt from yesterday, the same pants too. He moved; Salim followed. Salim had to walk faster than he usually did to keep up, and it seemed strange to him that the man should walk so fast. Salim walked faster now, getting closer to him. Ten paces from him. Now eight. Now seven. Salim felt excited, as if he were chasing a woman, as if this were some game and the man were leading him somewhere. Six. Five. The man shifted the suitcase to the other hand, and Salim slowed down, letting the distance stretch between them as if he and the man were two dots on a rubber band. They walked past the bank and the police station and then another bank. The man turned left. Salim turned left. The man climbed the steps into a building, and Salim halted nearby. He had never been here before. He entered hesitantly, climbed up the dark wooden stairs. Small shops, a mobile repair store, an electronics service center, a dried fruit store. One of the shopkeepers looked at him. "Are you looking for something?" he asked. Salim did not say anything. "I am asking you," the shopkeeper said.

"I had another man with me. He came up," Salim said.

"No one came here. Might have gone there." He pointed behind Salim. A coffee shop.

It was bright and warm inside the coffee shop. A long wall of just glass on one side. A young man walked up to Salim, and with a smile led him to a table. Not sure how to walk out, Salim felt lost. The man wasn't there. The waiter handed him a menu. Salim took it.

"You are wet, sir," the waiter said. "Would you like to dry yourself with a towel? The restroom is over there." He pointed at the other end of the café.

Boys and girls sat at the tables, laughing. A family sat at another table nearby; a group of men at another.

"I am waiting for someone," Salim said.

"Please," the waiter replied.

He should have asked about the man straightaway, Salim thought, asked if a man with a big suitcase had come here. Salim looked out from the immense glass pane that stretched along the entire wall. Drops of rain crashed against it and broke apart, leaving splintered little shapes on the glass. On the street below was a procession of cars stuck against each other and umbrellas, mostly black, but also red, blue, yellow, green, and some even painted with flowers and ducks. He had never seen the street like that even though he walked it all the time. Everything looked so different from above. Far away in the distance, he thought he caught a glimpse of the suitcase again. He got up, walked closer to the glass. It was him, walking this time with another man. Avoiding the attention of the waiter who stood nearby, he ran out, climbed down the stairs, and again rushed out into the street.

Now as he looked around, stranded on the street, the whole thing felt foolish. His hair was wet, his back was wet, and his limbs felt weak. It was too late to return to the godown, or the shop. A quarter of an hour had passed. He would receive nothing but rejection, or worse, even a scolding. He could have at least earned 300 rupees by now, and if he borrowed another 500 from Nazir, he would have had something to give at home. He was angry with himself. And yet he was waiting for the man to show up again. Salim dragged slowly toward Nazir's shop. He passed the ice cream shop, and today it made him angry. The man was there at the counter, Salim looked at him, but he was busy with a customer. If that had happened today, he thought, he might not have just walked away. In long raincoats that came down to their feet, soldiers stood on the streets, the dark barrels of their guns poking out through the collars of the coats. Salim imagined yanking the gun from the hands of one of them and turning the barrel at him, and pressing the trigger. Blood running with water beside the long overcoat. How long would he last? Two minutes? Five? Or maybe he could run into one of the alleyways and disappear. But the street was dotted with soldiers as far as he could see, their vehicles parked on the road, even more men in those vehicles. Farooq, he thought. Farooq. What must he have done at the end? Where had he been when they were killing Farooq? Barely aware of the road, of the rain, even the soldiers, he saw Farooq, laid out, the cotton in his nostrils, and in his ears, and dark bags under his eyes. His body intact except for the two holes at his chest. Fucking Farooq. Fucking Farooq. What must he have done at the end?

"Salim. Salim." He heard his name called. It was Khaliq at the cigarette kiosk. He had already reached his old market. He wanted to go away, not be here, but went on walking toward the kiosk.

"You forgot us completely!" Khaliq said. "By God, we keep remembering you here." They shook hands. Khaliq passed him a cigarette. "How is everyone at home?"

"Fine," Salim said. "How is your family?"

"The usual. Wife has run off to her father's again. Says she wouldn't come back to live with my mother. Mother also doesn't understand. The usual."

Salim remained silent.

"The flood is due. No?" Khaliq said.

"Yeah."

"You heard about Nazir?" Khaliq said.

"What about him?" A rock suddenly crushed Salim's chest and he knew that Nazir, too, was dead.

Khaliq gently touched his forehead with his fingers and pursed his lips. "Finished," he said. "Everything. Lost the shop. Gambled it away. They changed the locks."

Hearing little of what Khaliq said after that, Salim hurried away to see for himself. The rusted shutter down, two new big locks at the corners.

The other salesman at the luggage store shouted his name and came out to greet him. They hugged, and he brought Salim in. "Are you fine?" he asked. "Did you find a job? How is everyone at home?"

"Is it true about Nazir?" Salim asked.

"Yes," he replied. "Hasn't shown up in four days."

Just then the door opened, and the man Salim had followed all day walked in, trying to fit the suitcase and the umbrella through the narrow doorframe. Salim looked on as the salesman greeted the man. He greeted back. He looked at Salim, too, and then turned back to the salesman.

"You are an old store in the city, how can you keep your shop shut?" The man placed the suitcase on the counter. "My arms are falling off carrying this."

"When were we closed?" the salesman said.

"Yesterday. All afternoon."

"Oh yes, we were shifting stuff because of the rain," the salesman replied. "That is why."

"I went to another place too, but that too was closed."

"I am sorry," the salesman said. "What is with this old thing?"

"It doesn't open," the man said. "The children said they will open it, but they are too busy with nothing. They only say and do nothing."

The salesman began to fiddle with the lock. "What was the hurry in this rain, it could have waited," the salesman said. The man was older than Salim had thought.

"Who knows when something might be needed." He turned toward Salim. "But you young people only use things, and when they go wrong, you forget about them."

The suitcase was soaked with rain, the leather swollen dark brown.

"It doesn't look good," the man said, looking out at the street. "God should take pity on us."

"Here, uncle." The salesman clicked the suitcase open and swiveled it around to face the old man. "But you shouldn't have carried it around in the rain. It is leather. That damage is hard to cure."

The man did not seem to hear and was surprised at the ease with which the top lifted. The two large halves of the suitcase opened like an enormous mouth. The yellow silk lining inside was torn at places, tiny mothballs wobbled in a corner. He closed the lid and opened it again, and again, pleased at the sight each time.

Salim took leave of the salesman. "Do come again," he said as Salim was leaving. "I will tell the owner you visited. He was talking about you. Come again."

A fine rain fell outside. Salim pulled up the hood to cover his head. In the window glass smeared by the rain, the old man was still looking at the suitcase, opening it, closing it, and nearby, Salim's own reflection stood in the glass, the dark figure of his body in Farooq's jacket, and his face, hazily discernible, looking at him.

The Mannequin

THE MANNEQUIN ARRIVED LATE IN THE AFTERNOON. Wrapped in newspaper sheets, bound by jute strings. Mansoor immediately pulled at the strings, and the newspaper limply fell away. Pale and slender the mannequin stood, dark hair coming down its shoulders. He felt the sheen of the curls with his hand. Such soft, almost human hair. He noticed nothing wrong yet. What surprised him more than the hair were the arms that could move up and down. He dressed it with ease in a blue cotton kurta and, with some difficulty, since the legs wouldn't move, a white shalwar. The clothes fit and the colors would look even better in the sun. Holding it in the crook of his arm, Mansoor carried the mannequin outside and stood it in the empty left corner of the shop, in line with an old mannequin at the other end, arranging it so that the passersby could not miss it.

Twice he crossed the road over toward the cement shop and then walked back slowly, pretending to be someone else, a customer, a shopkeeper, his wife, the children. Even then he didn't notice anything wrong. What he saw was a beautiful woman standing before his shop, with shining human hair and clothes that fit perfectly, giving the place a new and welcoming presence, a distinction from all other shops in the market. The old faceless mannequin in the other corner was no comparison beside the new. But it too had served its purpose, one mustn't forget. How real the new mannequin looked, though, how real its face, how real the neck. How had they even made it? Must be molded from a cast using some machine, didn't they have machines for everything these days?

Only later, at the end of the day, when he carried it back inside in his arms, did he see it. The mannequin's face was inches from his own when he noticed its anguish. He thought that perhaps it was because of the strange angle at which he was looking at its face. That and the closeness, because closeness did sometimes make things appear strange. But what anguish!

Making space with his foot amid the scatter of small cardboard boxes, Mansoor set the mannequin down. He could have sworn it hadn't looked like that earlier. Even when he moved a step back, and then another, the face remained as it was, filled with agony, sorrow. Had he bought the mannequin for the full price, he would have called the seller that very moment and yelled into the phone, demanding the thing be replaced at once. But he had bought it at a fraction of the retail price, as a sort of gift from the wholesale dealer from whom he purchased garments, so he couldn't shout on the phone, couldn't make demands.

Four steps to the counter, four steps back to the wall, Mansoor paced about his small shop, looking sometimes at the mannequin from near and sometimes from the farthest corner. Anguish had set like stone into its face. The dealer, he was beginning to think, had sent him this thing on purpose, made him wait for a month and then sent this, and Mansoor knew why, not because he had got it at a reduced price but because he had been late in his payments to the dealer. Sure, he had been late, but he was a small neighborhood shopkeeper, not some fancy store owner in Lal Chowk. Didn't the dealer know what neighborhood shopkeepers made? Didn't he know that most of his customers did not even pay in cash, that he had to wait until the first of the month for them to settle their bills, and sometimes even the next? The dealer must have known all this and yet he had sent this weepy doll to his shop to ward off even the few customers he had. Suddenly, though, it seemed unlikely that the dealer would have looked closely at the mannequin's face, he who barely had time to look at the faces of living people. And also hadn't he himself been chasing after the dealer for a month now asking for the mannequin, and finally when the man had sent it, its price so cheap, how could he doubt his intentions? Besides, what did it even matter? Maybe it was just the light, maybe it would look fine again in the sun tomorrow. And even if this was what it looked like, so what! A mannequin was a mannequin, sad or happy or whatever, it would stand in the corner outside like the other mannequin. When was the last time he had even looked at that one?

A light, limbless bust on an aluminum stand, the old mannequin was harldy anything. He carried it inside now, his face inches from its smooth, pale, egg-like head, and he couldn't help looking. Without a face, without hair, its surface chipped where its nose should have been, it too began to look strange. He examined the pair together: one, with arms and legs, with a waist, with a human swell of breasts, and a face that looked sorrowful; and the other, a smooth, cylindrical thing, limbless and faceless, and yet suggesting the traces of a face, and now, beside the new mannequin, its face looked mournful too.

He walked home amid street noise and smoke and orange lights from cars, trying to think of other things, real things. It was a few minutes before seven. The barber was still open, the coppersmith was talking to a man outside his half-downed shutter, the tailor sat hunched over his sewing machine on a low table. Lights burned bright in the two pharmacy shops, busy with customers, but thankfully he didn't need to buy medicine for anyone tonight.

Fayaz's shop was shut, as it had been for months now. Its rusted tin signboard looked like scrap, as if it knew that shoes were not sold there anymore. Mansoor studied the shop's dusty shutter, trying to find any signs to suggest what the barber had told him earlier. He was struck by the size of the shutter, almost twice as wide as his own. Rumor was that Fayaz was opening up again, not a shoe shop but a fancy garment store this time, which made sense because Fayaz's father had sold some ancestral land for his daughter's wedding and some money might have been kept for Fayaz's business. Mansoor knew that a fancy garment store ten shops away would change things for him. His shop could no longer do without a full glass window, a door, big mirrors, and those bright lights that make things look better. Only then would he have some chance of surviving, when the customers could walk in and feel themselves inside a garment shop, taking their time as they looked at things, instead of standing on the road like they did now, making their purchases as if from some kiosk. It was, after all, the time of glass windows and bright lights, and if he did not move along with the world, he might as well sit in his shop and watch the world pass him by. He would need to collect money from his customers, though. He could tell them he needed it urgently; they would give it to him, at least some would; it was his, after all. His own debts, though, they would have to wait. But would the dealer, the goldsmith, the school really wait?

He stopped near Gulzar's fruit cart. A woman was buying melons, pressing on the round pale fruit gently with her fingers while her little boy kept pulling at her arm, pointing at something.

Gulzar winked at him. "Did you close, bigman?"

"Yeah," Mansoor said. "A little early tonight."

"Lucky man!" Gulzar said, giving the woman her change. "We poor leave at nine, after selling to bigmen like you."

The woman pulled at her boy, his unyielding feet skating along the road. "Tomorrow, tomorrow," she repeated, "I swear by God, tomorrow."

"What price the oranges?" Mansoor asked.

"These for sixty, those for eighty, and these ones for one hundred, for bigmen like you."

"A dozen," Mansoor said. "From these sixty ones."

"At least take from the eighty. What's wrong with you? What are you going to do with all your money?"

"Have it buried with me," Mansoor said.

Two at a time Gulzar put the oranges in the plastic bag. "But you won't give to the poor."

"One more orange," Mansoor said, holding out his hand.

"Why? Don't I have to make a living? I'm supposed to give away extra oranges now!" Gulzar handed him an orange. "I will charge this orange to your account."

Mansoor raised the orange on his fingertips. "Even a testicle is bigger than this."

"Then you should see a doctor," Gulzar replied.

Mansoor walked away, pressing his thumb into the skin of the small orange. Young men hung around the barbecue cart, their laughing voices carrying across the street, along with the pleasant smell of singed flesh. Embers glowed in their mirthful eyes. For a moment Mansoor was tempted to cross the road and have one of those skewers grilling on the bright charcoal, but it would cost the same as the dozen oranges. And last for what, two minutes? How strange that all good things were expensive. Inside his mouth, the last little slice of orange crushed and shattered, juicy, sweet.

HE WOULD HAVE PREFERRED to eat dinner later, but the electricity was going off at eight thirty, his wife said, and who knew when it would return, so they might as well eat and wrap up everything while there was still light. They had rice with kidney beans and turnips, and in a small bowl beside Mansoor's plate was the only little piece of meat, left over from yesterday. His mother spoke about the neighbors whose son had moved in with his in-laws, leaving his own old parents behind. He did not look at his mother but at the food. After she fell quiet, he thought of telling his family about the mannequin. But he wasn't sure, so he let it be. Then, as if reading his mind, his wife asked if the dealer had sent the mannequin or pushed back the delivery date yet again.

"No, he sent it," Mansoor said.

"He did?"

Everyone was looking at him, his mother, his wife, his daughter, his sister, and her two young daughters, with whom she had returned a year ago from her own in-laws'.

It surprised him that they should care so much about the mannequin. What had they to do with it?

"Is it like a real woman?" asked his eleven-year-old niece, the eldest of the children.

"No," he said, chewing, and feeling that he ought to say more. His daughter and niece looked disappointed.

"But you said that it would be like a real woman," his daughter said.

"When did I say that?" He began to feel a little annoyed, remembering vaguely that he may have.

"Outside, the other morning," the niece said.

"And upstairs too," the daughter added. "You said . . ."

"Quiet, girls. Let him eat." The grandmother cut them off.

ON TOP OF his wife later that night, his hand pressing in the dark against her mouth and her palm pressing against his, both letting out only soft groans while their daughter slept at the other end of the room, he suddenly remembered the mannequin's face. He turned his gaze away and kept going, his other hand gripping the wife's shoulder, her hand clasping his moist neck, her lips parting beneath his hand, but the face returned, clearer, not in the shop, not outside, but in the middle of a dark nowhere, the blue cotton kurta, the dark hair falling, lips pulled in a strange grimace, he kept going, going, his hand tightening around his wife's breast, her body becoming taut under his, their groans deepening, her nose, her lips, her eyes, going, going, till his wife's hand crushed against his mouth and his nose, and he let himself fall on her.

The room seemed enormous in the dark. He felt empty, distant. It was the eyes, something about the mannequin's eyes that was sad, maybe even its mouth. He really should return it, he thought, no good to keep a mourning mannequin in the shop, the shop that supported his house and family, it was a bad omen for the business, a bad omen for other things too.

"Mummy," the daughter whispered.

They remained quiet.

"Mummy."

"Kyah kyah?" his wife said in a startled voice, as if rousing herself from sleep.

"I am thirsty."

The mother remained silent. "Wait," she then mumbled, arranging her clothes. He switched on the little torch in his phone, and his wife stepped out, her hair flowing around her.

"Didn't I tell you not to eat so many turnips?" She picked up the glass of water from the windowsill. "The turnip ghost possesses you when you do."

Bending down and rising up, flitting across the ceiling and the curtain, a large shadow moved about on the wall, filling up the whole of it like some huge beast deep in the forest. By the time she returned and slid back in under the quilt, her husband had turned the other way.

"Can I tell you something?" she whispered. "Just listen, without getting angry."

"Let's sleep right now," he whispered back.

"Listen for five minutes. Then you can sleep."

"I know what you are going to say."

He knew he should not have said that, better not to have answered at all.

"How do you know what I am going to say?" the wife asked.

"Because we have talked about it."

"Who should I tell, then?"

"I just want to sleep. I am tired."

"You are tired?" she said. "What are you tired of? I spend my day here, not you. You leave in the morning and come back in the evening. I am dissolving away. From morning to night, morning to night, neither the donkey nor the owner happy. Everyone will build their own two rooms, but I will die in this house."

He remained silent.

"And to hear the words," his wife went on, "something or the other, something or the other, no matter what I do, something is always wrong. Am I not human?" She waited. "You will say nothing. No?"

"I am falling asleep," he said in a sleepy voice.

"Of course," she replied, turning away. "I should have talked earlier, at least you might have pretended to listen."

FAYAZ WAS STANDING on the roof of his shop, shouting at the vegetable vendor across the street. "No place for business, this. No place at all!" Standing beside the rusty signboard, he seemed in full spirits. Mansoor watched him from the street as he walked the children to school, carrying the younger niece in his arms.

"Where can we go, though?" the vegetable vendor answered. "Nowhere to go!"

"Closed today, open tomorrow, open today, closed tomorrow. A big bomb should fall on us!" Fayaz said. "The whole stink of it would vanish!"

He greeted Mansoor and the children as they passed beneath the shop. Mansoor greeted him back and the children looked up. "Study hard, girls," Fayaz shouted after them. "You should become a doctor, you a teacher, and you, little one, you an engineer, no, no, not an engineer, they are thieves, but so are the doctors and teachers."

Giggling and snickering, the girls kept on turning their heads to look back at Fayaz till they got closer to Mansoor's shop.

"Can we see the mannequin later?" his daughter asked as they passed the closed shop. "When we come back from school?"

"You said you would show us," his older niece added.

He pretended not to hear, but they asked again, pulled at his arms.

"It is broken," he said. "They will take it back and send a new one. Then you can see."

"What is broken?" the niece asked.

"Its leg."

"Which one?" asked the daughter.

They were both looking up at him, as was the younger niece in his arms.

"Right," he said.

"How did it bake?" the youngest one lisped, her arms around his neck, her face inches from his. She was looking at him carefully, like he was the child in her arms.

"It was broken when it got here," he said, avoiding her eyes. "But they will soon send a new one."

He greeted the school gatekeeper, put his niece down, and handed the girl her little schoolbag.

"Can we still see it?" his daughter and older niece pleaded. "Please. We will massage your hair this evening."

"Please. For two minutes," the younger niece said. "For one minute. Pleeease."

"Okay. Okay. You will. Go study now."

Their small mouths broke into wide smiles and their eyes shone. They walked away together, holding hands, in their long checkered shirts and white leggings, slowly getting lost among other little girls and boys.

THE MANNEQUIN STOOD where he had left it the previous evening. It looked even sadder today, as if its eyes were staring not at shelves filled with clothes in transparent bags but at some terrible sight. Mansoor could no longer bear looking at it. He turned it to face the wall, then carried the old mannequin out, dressed in its familiar discolored orange kurta, and set it up in its usual corner. Outside, cars, buses, scooters, auto-rickshaws honked away. The noise was worst at this time of day, worse even than in the evenings for some reason. Mansoor sprinkled water in front of his shop and swept gently with a broom. Dust rose in little puffs. So much dust. Every day, more dust, as if it fell from the sky. It hadn't been like this when he was younger, or was he too young then to have paid attention to dust? Now it was everywhere, and even though the garments in his shop were wrapped in plastic bags, the dust somehow found its way in, lining the edges of all the white clothes with soot. The new window would keep it out, though, at least some of it. He could see Fayaz still standing on the roof, talking to someone on the road.

HE SHOULD HAVE TAKEN an auto-rickshaw. Now it was too late. He was on the middle seat of the Sumo van, between two men on his right and a woman on the left. Behind were four more passengers, and in front, the driver, and a young man and a boy. Even with the windows down it was hot in the vehicle, and the mannequin on his lap was adding to the heat. He squeezed himself, as if apologizing for bringing on a fifth passenger where only three should have been sitting in this midday heat.

"Does she pay her fare too?" the driver asked, looking in the rearview mirror.

Mansoor smiled. "I will pay for her if you want me to."

"One can't just ride anywhere for free," the driver said. "Besides, she is all dressed up."

Mansoor saw how in the crowded Sumo it could resemble a real woman, dressed in the loose blue kurta and white shalwar from yesterday. He wondered if the driver could see the anguish in its face in the mirror. He should have brought the mannequin as it had come to him, tied up in newspapers, that was why the dealer had sent it like that, but for some reason he disliked the thought of bandaging it up.

"These days one is afraid to speak the truth," a man on the seat behind Mansoor's said, "but these things are strictly forbidden. Work of the devil."

Mansoor did not turn back to see who was talking.

"Nowadays dolls like this are all over the place," another man answered with jest in his voice. "Everywhere."

"So what?" the first man replied. "Let them be everywhere! Does a wrong become right if everyone does it?"

The mannequin weighed heavily on Mansoor's legs.

"On doomsday, man will be asked to breathe life into these images, these idols. What will he breathe into them then? Does man own his own breath, to breathe it into elsewhere? It is no joke . . . to create a human. Let them make it even more like a woman, but can any scientist in the world give it breath?"

With each word his voice rose, and the driver furtively lowered the music. The woman beside Mansoor kept looking out of the window, as if hearing nothing. It was quiet in the vehicle after that, till the man disembarked. Mansoor was relieved when the van set off again without him.

"There is always someone," a passenger at the back whispered.

"God forbid when there are two!" another replied.

The driver turned the knob. "This poor one, somehow going out! Where is she going, by the way?"

Mansoor smiled at the man, who was around his own age, maybe younger. "I am returning it to the dealer," he said.

"Why are you returning it? Is she not well?" the driver asked.

"Her hair is almost real," the man beside him said, touching it with his fingers.

"It is real hair," the man in the back answered, touching the hair gently. "You know those people who go around collecting hair, paying ten rupees, twenty rupees. For a handful of women's hair. It is big business. Lots of money."

MANSOOR GOT OFF before his stop, a distance to the dealer that could be walked, but he was not sure he wanted to walk through the crowded market with the mannequin on his shoulder. On other days the streets were full of prowling autos, vacant and inviting, slowing down as they passed you by, giving a view of their comfortable insides. Today they seemed to have disappeared.

Rather than calling the dealer and explaining on the phone, Mansoor thought it better to show up with the mannequin. What could he even have said on the phone? The dealer might have thought he was making a joke, but if he saw the face with his own eyes there would be no need to explain. Mansoor checked the mannequin's face again, to make sure that it still looked mournful. It did. He could simply ask for a different mannequin, the dealer could give him another date, that would be better. But now that he was standing on the street with the mannequin by his side, even getting to the dealer's was proving impossible. As if all the autos had gone somewhere. Strange that when you were really looking for something, that thing disappeared somewhere, and when you no longer needed it, it was all over the place.

People looked at him as he walked through the narrow lane crammed with pedestrians, and narrowed even more by the men and women who sat along the sides, selling wild mushrooms and brown eggs and dried fish, and the customers who stood around them in small groups. He saw one man nudge another to take a look at him carrying the mannequin, but Mansoor decided to behave as if he noticed nothing. So while people's eyes widened at the sight of him, or they smiled or laughed or murmured something, he looked straight ahead, holding the mannequin against him, as if he did not understand.

Two young boys were walking close behind him, so close that if he halted, they would knock into him. At first he thought they might be pickpockets, but there was nothing in his pockets and the boys didn't look like thieves either. But their presence so nearby made him uneasy. The mannequin slung across his shoulder like an overgrown child, Mansoor hurried up the crowded bridge. The boys were still only a step behind. He turned right, along the riverbank. They did too.

"What do you want?" he asked, looking over his shoulder.

"Nothing," one of them said.

"Walk on the other side, then."

"Why? Is this road yours?"

He stopped. Glared at them. They were young, one about his older niece's age, the other maybe a year younger.

"Walk," he said.

"You walk," the older one replied.

This angered him, but there wasn't much he could do. Telling from their clothes and rubber sandals, and their ease on this little side road in the middle of the city, he knew that they must live somewhere nearby, so to scold them was not a good idea. Besides, what had they done to him? They were just children.

"We are looking at your doll," the younger one said.

"Look from a little farther away then. You are climbing all over me!"

Stupid. This whole thing. Children were children, of course they would see the mannequin and be curious. It was silly of him to be carrying it. This was why the dealer had sent it wrapped. He turned back again; the boys were still there, following him.

"Uncle, uncle." The boys ran toward him. "You must be tired. Can we carry it for you?" They walked on either side of him now.

"No." He hastened his step.

"Please. Only up till there," they said, pointing toward the bend in the road.

"No." Any faster and he would be running.

"We will not drop it. Swear on my mother's life, we won't."

"Yes, please," the younger one added.

Not listening to them, he kept walking, as they kept pace with him.

"Where are you taking her?" the younger one asked, touching the mannequin's feet. The other touched its arm. Mansoor turned sharply, shouted at them. They were scared, but not enough to run away. He put the mannequin down on its feet, stared at them. His arms were tense. A few paces away, the boys stood their ground, looking at him, tentatively. "She is tall," the younger one remarked.

"What do you want?" Mansoor asked.

"We just want to carry it," the older boy said.

"We can walk beside you," the younger said.

Let them carry it, he thought. What's the big deal? It may be better for my back.

"Come," he said.

They walked a little wary, unsure what he had in mind.

"Hold it here," he said, placing the older boy's hands behind her neck. The other held her by the feet.

Together the boys walked, slowly, carrying the mannequin between them. They looked happy. Mansoor kept his hand under the mannequin's back, making sure that the loose hanging kurta did not touch the road.

"She is heavy," the younger boy whispered.

"If she was real, she would be even heavier," the older replied. "Wouldn't she?" He turned to Mansoor.

Mansoor pretended not to hear, and looked ahead toward the bend in the road, which seemed to have moved farther away. The boys carried the mannequin like a plank of wood, as it continued staring upward with open eyes. Its eyes looked different to Mansoor from this angle, as did the mouth, and while he was just getting a sense of this new face, and wondering if it still looked in pain, the boys suddenly shuffled and lifted the mannequin higher.

"Hey, hey," Mansoor shouted.

"This is really heavy," the boys said, resting it on their shoulders.

"Give it back then, give it back."

"Just up to the bend," the boys replied, holding the mannequin more tightly now.

"Rajaa, Sajaa, Tana." The boys called out names; they knew people here, it was their neighborhood. Mansoor looked around, but no children appeared.

"La ilaha illallah, la ilaha illallah," the older one began crying out, and the younger immediately joined, as if they were carrying a dead body.

"What are you doing?"

"Poor woman is dead," the younger boy said. "She was a good woman."

"La ilaha illallah, la ilaha illallah."

"Left behind three children at home," he said.

"And a husband. With a prick like a little finger." The older one held up his little finger.

Mansoor grabbed the mannequin by the waist. "Stop. Stop. Enough."

"Just up to the bend. You said we could go to the bend. We are almost there. We won't drop her."

The older boy ran his hand over the mannequin's face and breasts. The younger furtively grazed its knee. Mansoor yelled and pulled at the mannequin by its waist, but the boys did not let go. "Up to the bend, up to the bend," they chanted. Mansoor pulled harder, yanked it out of their hands with all his force, and watched, with surprise and horror, as the older boy reeled backward, holding a pale arm in his hands. The boy, too, looked in shock at the arm, and even before he fully came to a halt he dropped it near his feet and took off, looking back over his shoulder to see if he was being chased. Mansoor stood staring at the broken arm on the road. "Run, run," the older boy was shouting to the younger, who remained frozen in place near Mansoor, and just when the younger tried to run, Mansoor grabbed at his collar and swung his right hand against his face. The boy looked at Mansoor in a daze, and then he broke down crying, a thread of spit hanging from his mouth.

A woman shouted from a window above. A man ran out of a tailoring shop. A passerby appeared. Another woman was rushing toward them.

The tailor consoled the crying child, while another man restrained the older boy, who had rushed back and was trying to kick Mansoor. He, too, was crying.

"Aren't you ashamed?" said the tailor as he walked up to Mansoor. "Like a bull, hitting little children."

"You don't know what they did!" Mansoor said.

"Are you blind? He is a child."

"What did they do?" the woman said, grabbing the little boy by the wrist.

"Listen to me first. Listen."

"I am listening," the woman said calmly. "Tell."

"What can I say? I can't even say." Mansoor turned to the tailor.

"No, tell me," the woman said, anger rising as her voice cracked. "Maybe they have done something that deserves more than just a slap. One should know. Tell."

"You are like my sister," Mansoor said. "I apologize. I should never have raised my hand. I have children myself."

"Your children are fine," the woman answered. "No one will hit your children. It is my children who will be beaten, and it is not your fault. It is written in their fate."

"I said I am sorry," Mansoor said, again turning to the tailor. "I shouldn't have slapped him. They pulled at this mannequin and broke it."

"It was first written in their mother's fate, and I am bearing it, and now it is written in their fate too. Good for them."

The other woman, who had come down to the street, said that she had seen everything from the window of her home, that the boys had broken this doll, but he should still not have slapped the little child.

"Did you break this doll?" the mother asked her younger son. Tired from crying, he seemed not to hear. "Did you break it?" She shook the little boy by the shoulders. She slapped him harder than Mansoor had, on the same side of the face. The boy burst out crying. "Will you make me hang myself?" she yelled. "By God and the prophet, I will jump into this river. What do you want me to do? Where should I go? Should I hang myself? Should I set myself on fire? Will that make you happy?"

The other woman held her by the shoulders and pulled her away toward the steps of the tailor's shop, dragging her almost, her feet nearly lifting off the ground.

"The elder one is gone, out of my hands. Now the younger is going too. Let them go, let them fall under a truck, let a bullet hit them, let their kidneys burst, what can I do, what can I do!"

"They are children," the other woman said. "Don't curse them. A mother's curse can come true."

The mother sat on the steps of the tailor's shop. She did not reply. A girl brought her a glass of water.

Manzoor apologized again to the tailor, but the tailor hushed him. "I know," he whispered. "Children! Worse than dogs," he muttered as he tried to fix the broken arm back onto the mannequin. "You are lucky, though, you didn't hit the elder brother. Or he would have been lying flat on those steps right now, his nose full of blood, blood spilling everywhere."

No longer crying, looking far away, the woman was still on the steps, cradling the glass of water in her hands. The elder son sat near her. The younger stood a few steps away, leaning against the wall.

"A good amount of adhesive," the tailor said to Mansoor, "and the arm will be fine. Look, the crack won't even be visible under its clothes."

Neither the mother nor the elder boy noticed Mansoor as he walked past them; only the younger one, his hands behind his back, watched with still eyes. Mansoor wanted to walk up to him and apologize, he thought of touching the boy's head with his hand, but he was afraid, and walking past the boy, past his mother, past the handful of small shops with their shutters down, he neared the bend in the road. He knew he was not going to the dealer's, even if he could explain the whole thing he no longer wanted to go, and yet he kept walking, the broken arm in one hand and the rest of the mannequin in the crook of his arm, against him, no longer sure where he was going.

Frog in the Mouth

NO MATTER WHICH WAY YOU SIT, MY FRIEND, SOMETHING OR the other keeps aching. No? I mean, how you have been shifting in that chair. This leg over that, then that leg over this, then this one again, and then what? It is not you, my friend, that is all I want to say, it is not you. It is the chair. Time to accept that! And time also to accept that there is nowhere to go. Look around. All chairs the same! No? And between you and me, my friend, it is not even the chair. What then? you might ask. Well, that would need some thinking, and that is the one thing I refuse to do. Besides, the more you think, the less you understand. Wouldn't you agree? You look like a thinking man yourself. Not just the glasses, I mean even without them, even without the newspaper in your hand, I would know you to be a thinking man. Or maybe not! One can't be sure of anything these days. No? But please carry on with your paper. Do not let me disturb you. It is just that

I couldn't bear the sight of your discomfort. But you can safely ignore me. I blabber, that is what I do, and it means nothing.

But, maybe, it is our own sins. Who knows! I mean what could it be! Now I don't like to blame others. What is the point in that? Others are there to keep us under their thumb, to crush us under their foot, to cook a soup-quarter out of us. But what about us! You know what I mean? I mean even God seems to have forgotten us. No? And one can't really hold it against him. It is too much for anyone, and besides, doesn't he have other things to do than attend to this misery we have put together? But at least, my friend, at least we should have been sitting someplace else. Wouldn't you agree, someplace where the bulb doesn't burn right in your face, where you may still for a moment sigh in the shadows, where the air smells of the waters of heaven, you know what I mean, my friend, where drop by drop one could slowly forget this whole thing. Instead, here we are! In this grave of a tea shop, trapped on these chairs, reading news of our own death, choosing between tea and coffee. And it is no easy job to make a choice when the thing you want is not there. Or does that, in fact, make the choice easier? Well, that would need some thinking, and that is the one thing I refuse to do. But like I said, please don't let me disturb you. They pay no attention to me at my home as well, and how glad I am for that. They watch their TV and lay their little schemes, and what is it to me? Nothing, my friend, nothing. As long as I get my two meals, and a little from this and a little from that, thanks be to that God who has little say in anything anymore. But I must shut up now. I have disturbed you enough already.

I am not? Not disturbing! Are you sure? Well, thank you! That means so much! You agree! About what? Reading the news of our own death, trapped on these chairs. See! Aren't you a thinking man now? Picking up on a little thing like that. I like thinking people myself. Reading papers and counting money, if not their own, then other people's. But better still than the cattle walking around on hind legs, though I am one myself.

Do I read the papers? Unfortunately. One of my vices. That is how I begin my days, reading the papers and cursing my wife. But between you and me, I never win with her. And between you and me, let me also confess that I read the paper for the advertisements now. I mean, why not! One learns more there than from the news. What is being sold? What is being bought? Who is the new pimp in town? Congratulations, commiserations, all in there. If only one knows how to see. You know what I mean? I mean you read the news and the world seems to be on the brink of shutting shop, but then you look at the advertisements and everything is in place. Old shops shutting down, new shops opening. And isn't that what the world is about, my friend? It appears from your face, though, that you don't agree! Fair enough. I won't argue, but I feel you will come around, my friend. I am, after all, older than you, and years do matter, though it is also true that a fool remains a fool to the end of his days. He may at most become a respectable fool, and by God, how many fools can there be in one small place. Foolish fools. Clever fools. Wise fools. Stupid fools. Brave fools. Bloody fools. But that aside, my friend, I have this feeling that I know you from somewhere. There is a certain familiarity to your face, even the way you look at me now. It is a small city, after all. We might have hung by the same rail in some crowded bus once, or shared a boat across the river some evening, or walked off some afternoon alive from the same massacre. Who knows! You do take the boat often! See! I don't take the boat much myself. I can't swim, you see, and I can't walk over the water either, so I keep away. No one has the time these days to save anyone, and besides it is too much work. To take the phone out from the pocket, to take out the wallet then, then the other phone, and then the plunge into the dirty water. Too much! And what is the assurance that even if some brave savior does take the plunge, his things would remain where he left them? Even if there is little money in the wallet, even if the phone is a cheap one, someone always needs our things more than we do. Don't they? Wouldn't the savior hate the stupid sight of me then and wish he had paid no attention to the arms flailing in the river? And isn't the river already overflowing with arms, my friend? We wouldn't want to add these old limbs now, would we? But maybe we did meet in a bus! Now I have spent my time hanging by the handrails in all the wretched buses that crawl along this city, crammed blind in aisles like lambs, someone always mistaking your rump for their own. Lambs, by the way, reminds me that they serve some fine fried testicles here, and they have this walnut dip on the side. Now, is that delicious, my friend, or is that delicious! A neat little advertisement in the middle of mayhem. Oh, you haven't tried it! Well then, what can I say! Never walked into Nishat Bagh, say, never strolled into Shalmor, never smiled at someone while imagining their eyes rolled back forever. You are ignorant of a divine taste, my friend. For my first meal in heaven, by God, that is what I will ask of the angels. Whoever asks for whatever delicacies, I shall have my little plate of testicles. And can you imagine how things will taste there, my friend, everything so pure, so unadulterated, no worry of diabetes, no fear of blood pressure, no gout, no hemorrhoids, no fretting that someone behind our backs is always plotting our murder, the angels and fairies themselves ferrying our plates, smiling those beautiful ignorant smiles. But that we shall see there, my friend, for now we are here, and for a little bit of money we taste heaven, and I hope you are not one of those on whom God has shut the little doors of heaven. I mean do you eat testicles? You do, occasionally! Well, this is an occasion, my friend! And thank God the portions here are still large. Only you will have to shout for attention here even though we pay our good money. That fat otter at the counter, yes, he is a little hard of hearing, and the waiters wag their little tails in the master's misfortune, but between you and me, the bastard deserves every bit of it. Forty-seven years, forty-seven, not a joke. Never leaves you a penny. I came here the first time with a ten-paisa coin stolen from my father, ah how that poor man searched for it two whole days. Forty-seven years, never leaves a penny. Has his pockets full. Made money; here, there, everywhere. Your chair, for example. What plague would have them if they put a bit more wood into it, no, but how else do the rich become rich but by pinching the wood off other people's chairs, and once they become rich, my friend, what do they do, yes, they pinch whole chairs away, and God forbid if you happen to be sitting on the chair, my friend. But! One must be honest! He could make money, and he did! Good for him! If we could too, we would have as well. But all we could do was pass cannon fire. Please forgive my manners. But you know what I mean. I think you do, because you, too, like me, are a fool, my friend. Were you clever, you would have asked me to shut up a long time ago. Let me be the first to tell you that you are wasting your time listening to a madman. A certified madman. I have the papers to prove it. I can show you if you like. But you are a good person. I saw it the moment you walked in, and I knew that great God had heard my prayer. But send a curse on everything now and let us order. Better let me order on your behalf! To order things is half the pleasure. I would be glad to watch you eat. As if I myself were eating! But only if you want to, I wouldn't like to push you, not at all, and if my money wasn't stuck in the throats of those vultures, I would have bought it for us. Maybe next time. Well, here he comes, at last! Please remember him. Our crawling angel! The best waiter in this godforsaken hellhole! And don't you go by his face, he is a clever little fellow. Tastes everything along the way. Should I place the order then? Are you sure? Well then, a plate of testicles, my boy. You know how I like them, yes, just like that, a little more cumin and a hint of shallots, and the crushed red pepper! This gentleman is having it for the first time. His mouth should sweeten. He should refuse dinner at home tonight, and tomorrow he should be back with us. And don't forget the dip, my parrot, and don't make it runny with yogurt. Fly now!

And please forgive me, my friend, if I have talked too much. Please don't think I don't realize it, no one realizes it so painfully, but I cannot help it. It is my disease. Even Dr. Ali Jan said the same. You know who he was. Don't you? The Luqman of our time, the doctor's doctor; these kidney thieves nowadays are not worthy of tying his shoelaces. With his small eyes Ali Jan looked at me while I spoke, and I spoke, my friend, without pause, pouring out everything that ailed me, my heart, my liver, my kidneys, my eyes, my knees, in short, my friend, the whole machinery, and wise that he was, he listened, and then in a calm voice he said the trouble lay in my mouth. My tongue, he said, jumped around like a frog. Now that is called the eye of the seer. Tie your tongue, he said, and you shall be fine. But you won't, will you? I smiled. And of course this frog has been the ruin of me. But even the ruin comes from God, so thanks be to God even in these ruins. Which reminds me of an important question. Are you married? You are! Well, then you know! You have two children! Thirteen and ten! Then you know, then you know. And do you, by any chance, live with your mother and wife in the same house? You do! Well, I could see it in your eyes, my friend. You are a greater saint than those who hide away in caves, and your wife is a saint, too, and your mother is a saint, and if your father is still alive, he, of course, is a saint, and soon your two saintlings will grow up as well. All martyrs here, all saints, bearing on their shoulders clouds of sorrow and suffering and dreaming in their eyes the house, just a little bigger than the neighbor's, and of course a piece of meat to nibble on amid the fleetingness of this life, the transience of this world, tender, falling off the bone, with just the right spice, melting on the tongue. Ah, my friend, the mere thought has my juices running, let our thing come, and you will see, you will see, a pure pleasure, not like other things that one no longer understands. Do you ever feel like that, by the way, that you no longer understand anything? Not like you are trying to be wise, but you truly don't understand. I mean you think, This is the truth, this is the truth, and this truth falls on its ass and what appears false all along turns out to be the truth. Do you understand what I mean? I can't understand it myself. The fool you laugh at, he climbs the chair, and the horse you bet on sits all day on eggs. This is the world, my friend, and I can't make head or tail of it, and that is the beauty of God, that the whole thing makes no sense at all. And lo and behold! Here comes our angel. All conversation must cease! Please remember him, the parrot of this hell, and I hope he hasn't spilled tea in the saucer again. Did you check the salt along the way, my parrot? Now this is the scent, my friend, that makes the nose worth its trouble. Do you smell the cumin? And the whiff of the shallot? And the coriander? And the testicles themselves! Ah, the color! On my life, look! May this lamb be grazing the pastures of heaven right now. What else can one say! I can see you are excited, my friend. Wonderful. Let us begin. But please take some from my plate as well. No. No. I insist. I eat little but I eat good. Besides, this is not to fill the stomach, you know what I mean, for that a big pot must be waiting at home. And please do try the dip. The only person who made this dip so good was my mother, God have mercy on her soul, poor woman, searching for that ten paisa even when my father gave up. Mmmhhh, heaven, heaven.

I hope you are not tired of listening to me. I would be if I were you. But you don't really have to listen, you can keep nodding your head and think about your own misery. Even I don't listen to myself anymore. What for? The best way, my friend, is silence, but silence is not possible for me, because this frog keeps leaping, from one word to another, and one word to another, does not even let me breathe. It is not even a pleasure anymore, but a compulsion. I am convinced that if I keep quiet, my heart will stop, that it is the blabbering that keeps me going. And after all, is it not our sole blessing that we can talk, unlike the birds, fishes, dogs? Or maybe they talk as well. I am sure about the dogs, I hear them often in my neighborhood, complaining and scheming, and I know against whom. A very respectable man in our neighborhood who arbitrates everyone's dispute; may God save you from him, my friend, and may God save me.

You are getting up! Leaving? Already! How quickly you ate, my friend, as if this were a race, as if all the soldiers in this wretched place were after you alone. See, I am still at it. You must leave? Well, we were just beginning to know each other. But what can I say? You must what you must. Another five minutes wouldn't snuff out the world, I would say. It is going to rain! Is that why you are hurrying home? Well, let it rain, let it snow, let bombs fall from the sky like cabbages. It is all the same. No? Oh you are already leaving! Yes, yes, me too, a real pleasure talking to you. Let me stand up to shake your hand. And thank you, thank you for treating me to this balcony seat of heaven. Next time, it shall be on me. I insist. But I hope you find yourself unable to wait till then. You know what I mean. Oh, you are an engineer. Wonderful! Please forgive my asking, but have you engineers decided to turn this city into a nightmare? You are smiling, I like that. I really do. What do I do? Now that will take time to answer. Let's just say that I sit here, in this tea shop. For a living? Well, that is a separate conversation, my friend. Let me just say that I am a trader. I buy and I sell. What? Everything. Everything.

Acknowledgments

There are many people to thank for this book. Without some it would have taken even longer to write, and without some it might have been written too quickly, and it would for sure not have been whatever it is.

I want to first thank my parents, Rafiq and Asmat, who gave me everything they could, and let me take my paths.

And I want to thank my brother Khalid for the simplicity of his love and for his friendship.

I have been fortunate with friendships, meeting people who were warm, trusting, and true, and with whom I learnt much of life and living, and of politics, literature, and love.

Muzamil, Hilal, Rohail, Abir, Asgar, Javaid, Kavita, Zubair, Ishfaq, Idris, Alana, Hasan, Naseer, Uzma, Warisha, Auran, Frieda, Naveed, Feroz, Smita, Basharat, Waheed, Shoaib, Zeba, Afsha, Vijdan, Tatum and Asif and Sibtain always.

And Alice, Vivian, Elie, Arpita, Parijat Shahnawaz, Arshad Hussain, Ajaz Baba, Talal, Iram, Irfan Hassan, Vaibhav, Danny, Bashe'Baiy, Jamshed, Suvojit, Bashaarat Masood, Muzamil Mattoo, Saranga, Shahid Tantray, Setu, Zubair Dar, Athar, Azhar, Farris, and Anum Asi and Maazin.

I have also had the good fortune of meeting, along the way, teachers who were generous and brilliant and hopeful.

Zain-ul-Abidin, Jameela, Muzaffar Ahmad, Masooma Hussain, Muzamil (*again*), Fahein, Adam Hochschild, Vikram Chandra, Tim McGirk, Bob Calo, J. Robert Lennon, Michael Koch, Cathy Caruth, Helena María Viramontes, and Emily Fridlund (*who helped me see my own stories better*).

I am grateful to everyone at the Cornell English department for standing by me at a difficult time.

I would also like to thank Bard, Annandale-on-Hudson.

And thanks a lot to Tom Keenan who appeared just when I needed him.

I am indebted to my agent, Stuart Bernstein, who believed in these stories from the first moment and has stood behind them ever since.

I am very thankful to my editor, Masie Cochran, and to everyone at Tin House, for believing in this book and for making it better while allowing it to remain itself.

I am thankful to Archana Nathan at Penguin Random House India.

I want to thank Sangam House, Regional Arts Australia, and Association of Asian Studies and Swedish International Development Cooperation Agency (SIDA) for residencies and fellowships at various times during the writing of this book.

And thanks to Brad Morrow at Conjunctions and Adeena Reitberger at American Short Fiction. And to Krisna Uk, Elisabeth Weber and Clare Robinson. And Bashir Ahmad at the library.

And thanks also to Cremé for being a little oasis, and to Javed, Ishfaq, Mukhtar, Irshad, Farooq and everyone there.

I am deeply indebted to people I met during my years as a journalist, people who allowed me briefly into the inner spaces of their lives. I might no longer remember their names but their faces, their voices, their silences remain in me.

And, finally, to Shazia, for being there, always, the ground upon which I stand. And to Ali, who brought joy.

MUZAMIL MATTOO

ZAHID RAFIQ is a writer living in Srinagar, Kashmir. He was a journalist for several years before turning to writing fiction. *The World With Its Mouth Open* is his first book.